Gorgeous, feminine—untouched by trappings of fashion—the woman had a pure beauty. And babies. Three of them. One strapped to her front in a baby sack. The other two on either hip.

He wondered which of them was his niece.

He met the woman's dark brown eyes, taking in her impatience, the blond hair pulled back into a ponytail, the T-shirt and jeans. Her bare feet. "Can I help?" he asked over the crying, motioning to the babies in her arms.

"No," she said. She was bouncing her babies. One of which, the crying one, needed its nose wiped. *His* nose wiped, if the blue sleeper was anything to go by. "But as you can see, I'm busy, so—"

"I'm Rick Kraynick."

"Goodbye, Mr. Kraynick," she said, backing up enough to be able to close the door.

"Wait! Which one is Carrie?" He absolutely *had* to see his sister's baby, know she was okay, before he left.

Dear Reader,

Welcome to Harlequin's sixtieth birthday bash! And to THE DIAMOND LEGACY continuity! Four of us authors got together and planned one heck of a present to commemorate sixty years of sharing life with you through our stories. We had a great time making this happen—and, as we read one another's stories, we shed some tears, too. Because isn't that what life is all about? Being there for one another through the ups and downs.

In case you're wondering if I really believe this stuff, let me assure you, I do. I believe in the messages we send out with every single book: that love is truly strong enough to conquer all, that true love is real, powerful and all around us.

I picked up my first Harlequin Romance novel when I was fourteen. I was waiting in line with my mother at the grocery store. I was bored. There was a cardboard display of books. Take one free, it read. So I did. I read the book, too. And I read a Harlequin book a day throughout high school and into college. I told everyone who would listen that I was going to write for Harlequin Books someday. I majored in English in college so I could write for Harlequin. I ignored the condescending looks. The naysayers. I learned from the myriad rejection letters that Harlequin sent to me—letters where they always encouraged me even while they were telling me my work wasn't up to their standards. I never gave up.

It took six years, but I finally did get that call. They were buying my book! And this year marks the release of my fiftieth original title with Harlequin! An anniversary for me, too.

Readers, writers and the publisher that gives us all hope—we have a lot to celebrate.

Tara Taylor Quinn

A Daughter's Trust
Tara Taylor Quinn

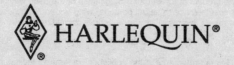

TORONTO • NEW YORK • LONDON
AMSTERDAM • PARIS • SYDNEY • HAMBURG
STOCKHOLM • ATHENS • TOKYO • MILAN • MADRID
PRAGUE • WARSAW • BUDAPEST • AUCKLAND

For Kelly Barney, a young woman who knows what
it means to open her heart to a new family member.
I am very, very proud to be a member of your
family. You are in my heart forever.

Recycling programs
for this product may
not exist in your area.

ISBN-13: 978-0-373-71584-8

A DAUGHTER'S TRUST

Copyright © 2009 by Tara Taylor Quinn.

www.eHarlequin.com

Printed in U.S.A.

ABOUT THE AUTHOR

With over fifty original novels, published in more than twenty languages, Tara Taylor Quinn is a *USA TODAY* bestselling author with over six million copies sold. She is known for delivering deeply emotional and psychologically astute novels. Quinn is a four-time finalist for the RWA RITA® Award, winner of a National Reader's Choice Award, a multiple finalist for the Reviewer's Choice Award, the Bookseller's Best Award and the Holt Medallion. Quinn recently married her college sweetheart, and the couple currently lives in Ohio with their two very demanding and spoiled bosses—four-pound Taylor Marie and fifteen-pound rescue mutt/cockapoo Jerry. When she's not writing for Harlequin and MIRA Books or fulfilling speaking engagements, Quinn loves to travel with her husband, stopping wherever the spirit takes them. They've been spotted in casinos and quaint little small-town antiques shops across the country.

Books by Tara Taylor Quinn

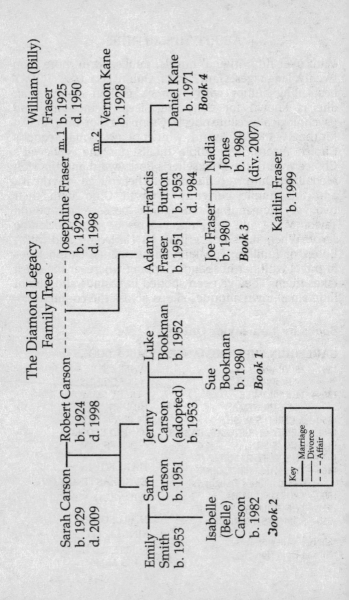

The Diamond Legacy
Family Tree

William (Billy) Fraser b. 1925 d. 1950

Vernon Kane b. 1928

Daniel Kane b. 1971
Book 4

Josephine Fraser b. 1929 d. 1998 m. 1 ... m. 2

Robert Carson b. 1924 d. 1998

Sarah Carson b. 1929 d. 2009

Adam Fraser b. 1951

Francis Burton b. 1953 d. 1984

Joe Fraser b. 1980
Book 3

Nadia Jones b. 1980 (div. 2007)

Kaitlin Fraser b. 1999

Jenny Carson (adopted) b. 1953

Luke Bookman b. 1952

Sue Bookman b. 1980
Book 1

Sam Carson b. 1951

Emily Smith b. 1953

Isabelle (Belle) Carson b. 1982
Book 2

Key
—— Marriage
—— Divorce
- - - Affair

CHAPTER ONE

GRANDMA'S FUNERAL WAS ON a Friday. Baby Carrie woke up with a stuffy nose that morning. Camden spat up his formula. Not a good day to leave them with a sitter.

But Sarah Sue Bookman had no choice. At home, alone with her kids, having a baby on each arm was relatively easy. The norm. She could do it in her sleep. Had done it in her sleep.

But inside the sacred walls of Saint Ignatius…with Grandma Sarah really gone… Having to say goodbye…

She had to leave the babies with Barb.

SITTING IN THE SECOND ROW of pews in the hugely imposing, historic San Francisco church, Sue could sense the ghosts of saints around her. In the Italianate architecture, in the candlelit altars lining both sides of the nave.

Approving? Disapproving? Did they know how angry she was? How unwillingly she was giving up Grandma to them?

She tried to focus on the priest, who'd known Grandma Sarah for many years, instead of on the open casket where her body lay.

Sue had expected this day to come eventually. Grandma was eighty years old. But it hurt worse than anything she'd imagined.

Maybe if they'd had warning. Maybe if Grandma had been sick for weeks or months, instead of a few days. Maybe then…

The pastor talked about Sarah Carson's generosity, her need to love everyone who came into her sphere—most particularly children. Just last week, when Sue had taken the babies on their regular visit to the house in Twin Peaks where her mother had been born and raised, Grandma had insisted Sue leave Camden and Carrie with her and hike a trail to the top of the peak. Something she'd been doing for as long as she could remember.

A hike she'd never take again. At least not from Grandma's house. Not coming home to iced tea and conversation with the only person she'd ever felt truly safe with.

Father John talked about the one child Sarah had borne, Sam, Sue's uncle. He was sitting in the front pew with his wife, Emily, and their daughter, Belle, who was two years younger than Sue.

Sarah had raised a fine man in Sam, the priest said, a man who could be relied on to lead the Carson family, to care for them, to carry on in the absence of his parents. With his car dealership that employed almost a hundred people, and his standing in the community, he was a testimony to the life Sarah Carson had lived.

And then the white-robed father looked at the

woman sitting next to Sue. He spoke of the infant daughter Sarah Carson and her now deceased, beloved husband, Robert, had adopted. Jenny.

Sue's mother.

Sue gave her mom's hand—glued to her with their combined sweat—a comforting squeeze as the priest droned on about Jenny's life as evidence of the mother Sarah had been. Sue's father, seated on the other side of his wife with his arm around her, tightened his embrace, and rubbed the side of Sue's arm with the back of his hand at the same time.

That's how it had always been with them. Jenny and Luke together through every step of life, keeping Sue firmly within the bonds of their love.

Sue loved them. Yet she'd entertained the uncharitable thought, often enough for her to write her own sentence to hell, that if Jenny had had her way, all three of the Bookmans would dress like triplets.

All the time instead of just the vacation shirts. The Bookmans Take Manhattan. The Bookmans Do Hawaii. The Bookmans Visit Mickey.

When the Bookmans flew to Italy—The Bookmans Roam Rome—Sue had refused to wear the shirt. She would never forget her mother's crestfallen expression as they'd left the house early that Saturday morning on their way to the airport.

She'd been nine at the time.

And she'd called Grandma Sarah from a pay phone at the airport in lieu of visiting the bathroom as she'd said she was going to do.

Grandma had told her she'd be embarrassed to wear the shirt, too. And she'd reminded Sue that Jenny loved her and only wanted what was best for her family. "Just follow that big heart of yours, my girl, share it, and you'll be fine."

It had sounded so easy.

When, in truth, nothing ever was.

"I'LL BE RIGHT BACK, Ma. I need some air."

How many times in the past twenty years, since that first rebellion back when she was nine, had Sue made excuses like that? *I need to use the restroom. I'm going to the water fountain. I'll be right back....*

As usual, they earned her the same concerned and loving look—a glance from her mom that effectively shut out all of the quiet voices floating around them in the crowded vestibule outside the church sanctuary. "You okay, baby?"

Nodding, Sue gave her mother a hug. "I'll hurry."

"How's Belle? I saw you talking to her."

"About like me. In shock. Can't imagine life without Grandma." Sue glanced over to where her cousin was standing with her mother and father, just as Sue was.

As it had always been.

Sam and Emily with Belle attached to Emily's side. Luke and Jenny with Sue right next to her mother.

All that was left of the Carson family.

Some of Sue's best childhood memories had been at Grandma Sarah's house when the adults would be involved in whatever adults did around the table, and she and Belle could escape.

Sue from claustrophobia. Belle from her father.

"I won't be long," Sue whispered quickly now as one of Jenny's longtime high school friends came up to offer condolences and ask how long she and Luke were in town.

Glad for the chance for a breather without having to leave her mom and dad unattended, Sue bolted out into the cool March air.

As THE GROUNDSMEN lowered the cheap box into the public grave, he stood back, watching, but vowing not to feel. Not to try to understand.

If any mourners had attended the funeral, they'd since left.

Except for the lone onlooker who stood by the grave. A young black woman. A friend?

That he'd had a little sister he'd never known was not a surprise to him. The fact that his drug addict mother had been able to carry a second baby to term was a mystery. But that she'd been permitted to keep the girl—that, he could not comprehend. What kind of society, what kind of child services system, had allowed a mother already proven unfit to teach her daughter the ways of drugs and sex instead of ABC's?

The fact that the child—a woman of sixteen—was dead, had killed herself, didn't cause the twitch that suddenly appeared at the side of Rick Kraynick's eye.

The fact that he cared did that.

THE BURST OF BRISK AIR didn't alleviate Sue's claustrophobia as she stood on the steps of St. Ignatius. She had to get away. To take in long clean breaths of ocean breeze. To hear the waves as she watched them crashing to shore and rolling out again.

Grandma Sarah had promised she'd live forever.

Grandma, the one person who'd never judged her. Not that she'd known everything about her granddaughter. Some things no one knew. Or would ever know.

Sue's secret. Buried. Just like Grandma.

"Hey."

Recognizing the voice, Sue glanced up. "Joe! Hi." She'd phoned him. Left a message. She hadn't expected to see him, even though he'd been her best friend all through high school. The only best friend she'd ever had. But high school had been a long time ago.

Before she'd emasculated him.

Now he was mostly just her boss.

Besides, he'd never met Grandma.

"Your message said one o'clock. Is it over?"

"Yeah. There's no graveside service since her ashes are to be stored with my grandfather's in the family vault. Mom and Uncle Sam are having a meal catered at Grandma's house in Twin Peaks, so we're heading there next. Would you like to come?"

"I should get back to work. I only stopped because I was in the area."

Bosses didn't often stop by churches where employees' family funerals were taking place.

Old friends did.

"It would really help to have you there," Sue said, afraid her composure was going to desert her completely.

How in the hell was she going to be able to walk into the house her grandparents had had built back in 1946, and lived in for sixty-three years, without Grandma there?

There'd never been a gathering at the house without Grandma.

Hunched in his trendy, expensive trench coat, Joe stared at her for an uncomfortable moment. And then nodded.

"I can ride over with you, if you'd like," Sue continued. "Since you don't know where she lives." And then, feeling another unexpected stab through her heart, she added, "Lived."

He didn't meet her eyes a second time, but his nod was enough. Joe knew her. He understood.

Right now, he was the only tie to sanity she had.

"THANK YOU FOR THIS."

Glancing at her as they pulled onto Grand View Avenue—a street with eclectic and colorful million-dollar, postwar homes, a street known for its magnificent views of the city and not for it yards, which were almost nonexistent—Joe merely shrugged.

He'd changed so much from the open-hearted boy she'd known, Sue hardly recognized him these days.

"Seems strange, after all this time, for you to meet my folks."

In her youth, she'd kept him hidden. He'd been her prize. The one part of her life that was solely hers. Until he'd wanted more than friendship. And while she'd been able to give him love, she'd backed out of sex.

Joe grunted. As he found a spot to park in the street just beyond Grandma's house, he added, "I won't be able to stay long." He didn't crack a smile.

She wasn't responsible for his divorce. Nor could she get him more time with the daughter she knew he adored. Those hurts had come long after she'd done her little number on him.

"Last week when I called the office, Thea said that you were with your father." People were going into Grandma's house. Some Sue recognized. Some she didn't. Heart pounding, she wasn't ready to join them.

Joe didn't comment. She studied him, his close-cropped black hair, his crooked nose and his line-backer body.

"Is he still in town?" She might not get another chance for personal conversation with him for a while. She cared about him.

Besides, Grandma wasn't in that house at the base of the famous Twin Peaks, wasn't welcoming her guests.

Joe shrugged.

"How long's it been since you'd seen him?" During their four years in high school she could only remember a brief visit from Joe's fisherman father, who'd come down from Alaska for one of the holidays. The checks he was supposed to have sent to his mother, who was raising Joe, were only a little more frequent than his visits.

"A few years."

"So he knows Kaitlin?" Joe's ten-year-old daughter.

"They've met a time or two."

"Was he here just to see you?"

"So he says." The dry tone revealed more than the coldness in Joe's eyes. "He's been in town a couple of months."

"Did he stay with you?"

"No."

"Why do you think he came?"

"Money?"

"Yours?"

"I'm not aware of anyone else he knows who'd let him sponge off of them."

"How much did he ask for?"

"None."

"You gave it to him before he asked so he'd get out of town, right?" It was what this new, emotionally closed Joe Fraser would do. Joe Fraser, commercial real estate broker, loner.

"I'm not giving the man one red cent."

"And he left without it?"

"No."

Frowning, Sue tried to decipher that one. Did that mean Adam had found a way to get the money without asking? That someone else had given it to him, after all?

Or that he hadn't left?

Her mom and dad parked their rental sedan across the street. Jenny stumbled as she got out of the car, and Luke hurried around to help her, steadying her with an arm firmly around her back. His gaze met Sue's. He whispered something to his wife and they both smiled over. Waved.

Sue waved back and Joe turned to see who was there. She had to go in. They knew she was out here. They'd come looking for her. She swallowed.

"Is your dad still in town?" she asked Joe, instead. Their conversations were generally short-lived, over the phone and strictly about business. Specifically, the books she kept for him.

Joe replied with a brief nod.

"Has he said how long he's staying?"

"For good. Are you going in there or not?"

A fresh wave of panic washed through her. "You're coming, aren't you? Just to meet my folks?"

He hesitated and Sue was afraid he was going to refuse. Then he opened the car door.

"WHO WAS THE HOTTIE?" Belle asked. "Someone new you forgot to tell me about?"

Joe had met Sue's parents, a polite, uneventful moment considering all of the effort she'd taken in high school to keep them away from each other. And then, making sure they could take Sue home before heading back to their hotel in the city, he'd excused himself.

Sue gave her cousin as much of a grin as she could muster and shook her head. "That was just Joe."

About sixty people were milling around Grandma's huge living room, spilling over into the formal dining room and out onto the deck. Her mom and dad were there somewhere. Uncle Sam and Aunt Emily, too.

A lot of the rest Sue didn't know.

"Joe Fraser?" Belle asked, as they watched people from their vantage point at the foot of the white-banistered curving staircase that led to the three bedrooms upstairs: Grandma's room and, at one point, Jenny's and Sam's.

"Yeah."

"Ah…" Belle sipped the wine she'd poured from a bottle out of Grandpa's rack on the wall opposite the fireplace. "*The* Joe," she added. "I didn't realize you guys were friends again."

"We aren't. We're friendly, but that's about it. Joe hasn't confided in me in years." She sipped from the glass Belle had poured for her. "If not for the fact that he needed a bookkeeper when I needed a job that would allow me to stay at home with the babies, we probably wouldn't be in touch at all."

They'd made their peace. She'd just never again been welcome in the inner circles of Joe's heart.

"It's a shame," Belle said. "He's gorgeous. Available. And you guys were such good friends."

"Joe's changed a lot. And besides, I've never been in love with him. Not in that way."

Belle nodded, and Sue knew she understood. Belle had recently gone against her overbearing father's wishes and broken up with the man her dad had wanted her to marry. Try as she might, she hadn't been able to fall in love with the young lawyer.

The sound of a glass shattering on Grandma's hardwood floor made Sue wince. She moved toward the sound, intending to clean up whatever had spilled before it had a chance to soak in, but saw Aunt Emily had got to the mess in the dining room first.

"I've already done some checking and found that on average, it's taking homes a year or more to sell…"

Sue froze, just around the corner from the voice. Her uncle Sam's.

"So you're planning to sell?" She didn't recognize the other voice. It was male.

"Of course. What would I want with this old thing?"

"Nadine and I wondered if perhaps you and Emily would move into it. The place is beautiful. And the views exquisite."

They were talking about Grandma's home.

"God, no! I wouldn't live in a seventy-year-old house. I want copper pipes and insulation that works."

This is your mother's home, you jerk. His childhood home. Not that sentimentality had ever mattered one whit to Uncle Sam.

"So it is going to you, then?" The other man continued to butt in to family matters that were none of his business.

"Of course." Uncle Sam's voice boomed with confidence. "We meet with the attorney this week, and I'm sure I'm executor of the estate. I am Robert and Sarah's only biological child. Their only heir."

"Oh!" The other man's surprise was evident. "I didn't realize…I mean, Jenny's always…"

"Been adopted," Sam said drily. "I am the only true Carson and I know my father well enough to be sure that while he'll have taken care of Jenny, the bulk of the estate will come to me…."

"Oh, God, Sue, don't listen to him."

Sue jumped as Belle spoke just behind her. Her cousin put a hand on her arm, resting her chin on Sue's shoulder. "He's an ass. It means nothing...."

"He's right," Sue said. "He is the only Carson by blood."

"So?"

"I never realized he resented my mother so much."

"He resents the world because he's not God," Belle said, mimicking her father's tone.

Turning, Sue met her cousin's caring gaze. "Did you ever resent me, growing up?" she asked. "I was two years older, and so close to Grandma. And your dad's right, you had blood ties. I didn't."

"As if it mattered," Belle said, flipping Sue's ponytail affectionately, "to anyone but him. And I was as close to Grandpa as you were to Grandma." They walked toward the kitchen—and relative peace. "The only thing I resented about you, my dear, was that you had parents who really loved each other. And you."

Sue could have placated Belle with meaningless words, but they both knew the truth. Emily Carson loved Belle with all her heart. At one point, she'd probably loved Sam that way, too.

But somewhere along the way Sam Carson, the heir apparent and new head of the family, had become one very difficult man to love.

CHAPTER TWO

THIRTY-ONE-YEAR-OLD Assistant Superintendent of Schools Rick Kraynick was slowly getting used to eating alone. Living alone.

Thinking alone.

What he didn't usually do was drink alone. Or drink, period. He'd seen firsthand what substance abuse could do to a person. And while there were days, too many of them if he was honest with himself, when he didn't much care about his health and well-being, he wasn't going to be a burden to society.

So he should have felt right at home at the Castro Country Club Friday night. On 18th Street, the club wasn't far from Twin Peaks, one of Rick's favorite jogging spots in his younger days. And a favorite picnic place for him and Hannah....

Look out there, Daddy. You can see the whole world from here!

Nodding to the folks—mostly men of varying ages—hanging out on the faux marble steps leading into the old white Victorian mansion whose first floor housed the Castro Country Club, Rick tried not to let his mind wander. To think beyond the moment. The current goal.

He'd spent the afternoon trying to find the woman who'd given birth to him. She wasn't at the address he had for her. No one had been home in the place where she supposedly rented rooms. Her phone service had been shut off—again.

He had no idea where she was working. If she still was. Just because Nancy Kraynick had had a job last week didn't mean she'd still be employed today.

The older woman who'd been hanging clothes out at the house next door had eventually suggested he check "the club" for his mother. After some prompting, and a five-dollar bill, she'd remembered the name of the place.

Turned out Castro House was a coffeehouse that held substance abuse recovery meetings. And offered former addicts a place to hang out and talk, to bond with others fighting the same battles.

What she hadn't told him was that it was largely a gay men's establishment. Which might be fine for his female mother. Rick, on the other hand, was pretty certain, by the glances he was receiving, that he was raising false hopes. His instincts telling him to get the hell out, he approached the espresso counter and ordered a mocha he didn't want.

Luck would have it that this Friday, because he'd taken the day off and was on a mission, he was sporting a pair of worn, close-fitting jeans. With a long-sleeved cotton baseball shirt that had seen too many washings.

He'd been going for comfort. And no flash.

In this place, tight-fitting clothes—no matter how old, were flash.

Paying for his coffee, pretending not to see the smile the volunteer barista bestowed upon him, Rick turned, taking in as much of the room as he could without making eye contact.

As far as he could tell, his mother wasn't here.

But then, it'd been years since he'd seen her. Would he even recognize her?

"Have a seat…." A man about Rick's age pulled out the second chair at a table for two.

"Uh, thanks, but…I'm looking for someone," he said, sipping too quickly. He burned his tongue.

"Who?" the casually dressed man asked. "I might know him. We're all pretty friendly around here."

"Nancy Kraynick. You know her?" Not that she was probably going by that name now. After all, it was only her legal designation, which didn't seem to compel her to actually introduce herself that way. Growing up, he'd heard her called many different things. Some not so nice labels.

"Yeah," the guy said, surprising Rick. "She's been a regular around here, on and off, for the past couple of years." Rick had to wonder, was Lothario telling the truth or just looking for an opening?

"Have you seen her today?" Rick asked.

"No. But then I just got here. You a friend of hers?"

He couldn't bring himself to claim even that close an association. "No."

The man's eyes narrowed. "You aren't some john,

are you? Because I have to tell you, she's through with that. Has been for some time. So if you're looking to get something from her, you'd best try looking someplace else."

Protectiveness? From a man...toward Rick's mother?

This guy must not know her well. He hadn't had time to see that her lies were only skin-deep.

His mother always had been able to spin the most believable yarns. Especially believable to a young man who'd adored her and needed badly to believe she would straighten herself out and make a home for him. With her.

Problem was, Nancy Kraynick's yarns had always become tangled in the knots of drug abuse, and in alcohol stupors that went on for months.

"No, I'm not a john," he said now, biting back his disgust at the woman his mother was—a woman who'd had johns to ask about.

The pretty man frowned. "She's not in trouble, is she?"

"Probably, but that's not why I'm here."

The guy studied him and then pulled out the empty chair. "You look troubled," he said. "Have a seat. Maybe Nancy will show."

"No thanks." Rick couldn't even pretend he had an appointment, pretend he'd stay if he could. Five minutes and he'd had enough of this place.

There were other ways he could find out what he needed. He had a name and address of someone who could probably help him, thanks to Chenille Langston, the young black girl who'd stayed behind after Christy's small funeral. The name and address of a woman who apparently had another Kraynick in her care… A name and address he shouldn't use. And he had official options, too, which would inevitably involve red tape— and probably require evidence of things that might take a while to prove.

If what he'd been told at the cemetery this morning was true, his whole life was about to change. Again. He needed information. Confirmation. His mother had seemed the obvious source. Stupid of him to think his mom would ever—ever—have answers for him.

An hour later, standing in his en suite shower in the Sunset district home he'd shared with Hannah, Rick scrubbed until his skin stung.

Then he stood, leaning an arm against the wall, head bowed, as he let the hot water cascade over his back.

A year ago, life had been great. He'd been the single dad of a great kid, with a world of possibilities ahead for both of them. Tonight he was the son of a druggie; the older brother of a dead sister he never knew about; a grieving father.

They'd told him it would get easier. That as time passed, the violence of the grief raging through him would lessen.

They'd lied.

MOST OF THE CROWD WAS gone by nightfall. Sue slipped upstairs, to call Barb, from the bedroom she'd always slept in on visits to Grandma.

"I'm finished sooner than I thought," she said,

keeping her voice low, for no logical reason. Old habits, conditioning—a need to keep her private life private—died hard. "I'd like to swing by and pick up my brood."

Emily and Belle were in the kitchen, overseeing the caterers. Uncle Sam was downstairs, too, probably in the living room, cataloguing his take. Or checking that no one had taken anything yet. Not until he directed who would get what.

"Wilma called. She told me to keep them all night, no matter what you said. You need this night to yourself." Barb's tone was sympathetic. "Besides, they're already asleep."

Glancing at her watch, Sue realized it was after nine o'clock. Far too late to be making this call. Wilma, a foster care supervisor, was right. Sue wasn't ready to take up motherhood again tonight.

"I'll be there first thing in the morning," she said, missing the young charges in her care. Missing the busy-ness, the unconditional acceptance of love. "Don't worry about breakfast. I'll get them early enough to feed them at home."

Closing her cell phone, sliding it back into the case at her hip, Sue took the deep breath necessary to go back downstairs—but stopped. Someone was upstairs. Crying.

Following the sound down the hall to Grandma's room, Sue pushed open the door. Her mother, sitting in the off-white Queen Anne chair in the corner by Sarah's bed, had her face buried in a nightgown she'd given Grandma for Christmas.

"Hey." Sue fought her own tears as she knelt at her

mom's feet. "Come on, you shouldn't be up here alone."
She'd said the first thing that came to her mind, though
there was no reason why Jenny shouldn't be visiting her
own mother's room.

Jenny started, clutching the hand Sue placed on her
knee. "I…she was…I loved her so much," she said.

"I know." Tears filled Sue's eyes and she could
hardly speak as her throat closed up. "Where's Dad?"
she managed to ask after a moment.

"In the bathroom."

Sue's gaze followed her mother's around the room,
taking in the long dresser covered with tiny antique
perfume bottles on top of doilies Sarah had stitched
herself. The collection of miniature porcelain animals.
The tall bureau that had been her grandfather's, still
holding his key valet and an encased Giants baseball
he'd caught on a fly at a World Series game.

"Not once in all my years growing up did they ever
make me feel as though I didn't belong to them,"
Jenny said.

And that's when Sue realized. "You heard Uncle
Sam, too."

"It's not like he's ever tried to hide how he feels,"
Jenny said. "I love my brother, Sue. I see the insecurity
behind all of his blustering. I just wish he'd see that I'm
not and never have been a threat."

"I can't stand to be in the same room with him," Sue
said. "He's just plain cruel…."

"Everything he says is true."

"That everything here belongs to him?"

"That he's the only true Carson child."

"Mom! I can't believe you're saying that! We belong here as much as he does."

"And what we care about, the things that were dear to Grandma and Grandpa, the pictures, the things that hold memories, Sam won't want, anyway. It's going to be fine, honey. I can't let him upset me like this."

"Who's upsetting you, Jen?" Luke came into the room and Sue stood, giving her father a hug. Her parents had flown in from their home in Florida two days before. They'd been in town over Christmas, but she'd missed them more than usual this time around.

"Sam," Jenny answered.

"Well, then that makes three of us he's getting to, huh?" Luke pulled his wife to her feet, an arm around her and one still around Sue. "How about the Bookmans go face the dragon together?"

HEART POUNDING Monday morning, Rick listened to the phone ring. Once. Twice.

Come on, he willed Ms. Sue Bookman—the faceless woman who, at the moment, meant more to him than anyone else in the world.

A third ring. And a fourth.

Answer your phone.

He didn't know her age, her race or her marital status. He just knew she held his future in her hands.

And that she lived just outside the Bay Area.

The Internet phone listing matched the address he'd been given at the cemetery.

"Hi, it's me. I'm probably changing diapers. Leave a message and I'll get back to you."

She was changing diapers.

"Sue, my name is Rick Kraynick. I'm assistant superintendent of Livingston schools...." He wanted her to know he was a good guy. Trusted around children. "I have an urgent matter to discuss with you. Please call me as soon as possible. Thank you."

There. That should do it.

Sitting back at the huge, glass-topped desk in his corner office on the fourth floor of the district building, Rick almost smiled. He'd made the call. Nothing was going to stop him.

CHAPTER THREE

GRANDMA'S ASHES WEREN'T even in the vault before Sue's uncle arranged the meeting for the reading of the will. He'd said his urgency was out of respect for Jenny and Luke, who had a home in Florida to return to, but Sue didn't buy that for a second.

Sam Carson, in an impressive gray suit, paced the foyer of the high-rise building that housed the lawyer's office more like an expectant father than a grieving son.

"Mom said he's been chomping at the bit all week-end," Belle whispered to Sue as the two stood together on Tuesday morning across from the reception counter, much more casually dressed, in good pants and blouses, in a quiet corner of the high-rise entryway. They were sharing a cup of bad coffee neither of them wanted while they waited to be called to the first-floor office. Sue held the cup while Belle gently bounced Camden up and down, soothing the little guy back to sleep.

Baby Carrie was good for another hour, snoozing in the pack on Sue's back.

Jenny and Luke had not yet arrived from their hotel a short walk down the street.

"Thank goodness Stan Wilson's not here yet," Sue whispered back when Sam stopped to say something to his wife, who was sitting on a chair in the opposite corner, reading a magazine. "At least Mom and Dad won't be blamed for making your dad wait."

Stan Wilson had been handling Grandma's affairs for only a couple of years. Their longtime attorney, Mitch Taylor, had retired shortly after Grandpa's death.

Sue wondered if Mr. Wilson had met Sam Carson yet.

"Dad makes me sick," Belle said. "It's not like he needs any of Grandma's money."

"Maybe he'll relax a bit when he's officially God Carson," Sue said, then bit her tongue. After a long talk with her parents Friday night at their hotel—where she'd opted to sleep over rather than have them drive all the way out to her place—she was supposed to try her best to love her uncle. Her mother had always insisted that Sam loved all of them. He just had…issues.

Well, so did the rest of them.

Of course, it was a little easier for Jenny to be understanding these days. She had Luke as a buffer. And they lived in Florida. Out of Sam's reach.

Sam didn't mess with Sue, either, but she sure hated to see how much grief he gave Belle.

And Emily.

Sue's phone vibrated against her hip. Juggling the coffee in one hand and the stuffed diaper bag on the opposite shoulder, she checked to see who was calling.

In her business, she never knew. The state might

have someone who wanted to see one of her charges. More importantly, they could have an emergency and need someone to take a baby immediately.

Which was why she had her home phone calls forwarded to her cell anytime she was away.

She didn't recognize the number.

But because she didn't want to get stuck making small talk with her uncle, who was heading toward Belle, Sue listened to the message.

She didn't know any Rick Kraynick, assistant superintendent of Livingston schools.

Had never heard of him.

He wasn't from child services....

The revolving door from the outside spun around. From behind the pillar practically blocking her from the cold air, Sue could make out two people, not her parents. Both were tall. And broad. And...

"Joe?" she called out, sliding her phone back into its case. She walked over, taking in the man at her boss's side. He was older, in his fifties, Sue would guess. Gray hair. With eyes that, while not the same dark blue as Joe's, seemed equally impenetrable. Another strong, silent type?

"What are you doing here?" she asked. Weird that he'd show up on the very morning she was waiting to hear Grandma Sarah's last requests.

"Business," Joe said, guiding her away from the other man without any acknowledgment whatsoever. As though he wanted to make sure they didn't meet. "A nine o'clock appointment. How about you?"

"Me, too," she said, feeling awkward standing talking to him with a baby on her back. Joe didn't seem to notice. "Nine o'clock."

Even after several years of working for him, of being peripheral acquaintances, she still had trouble with the new Joe. She missed her friend. More this week than usual. "Grandma's will is going to be read."

He frowned. "I'm here for a will, too."

"Oh!" Sue's hand found its way to his arm before she could worry if she'd offend her employer. "I'm sorry," she told him. "Who died?"

"It's not for me." Joe glanced back to the man who'd come in with him. Dressed in a beige trench coat, with shoulders hunched up to his ears, the older gentleman had spoken to the receptionist and was standing alone in the foyer, apparently in a world of his own. "I'm just here with him."

"Who is he?" she asked. But she thought she knew. The eyes might be different colors, but there was something so…alike….

"My father."

The infamous Adam Fraser. "He's a lot more muscular looking than I pictured him," she said, trying not to stare. There'd been a time when she'd wanted five minutes alone in a room with that man.

A time when she'd thought about writing to him, begging him to come home to his son.

A time when she'd hated him for all the pain and rejection he'd put Joe through.

"Comes from years on a fishing boat," Joe said drily. He had his back to the man. "Who's that?" he asked, nodding to her right.

Sue turned. Smiled at her cousin's curious stare. Sam had moved on. "Belle."

"Your cousin. She's a couple of years younger than you."

He'd remembered. "Right."

"Is the baby hers?" Camden was sleeping, snuggled against Belle's chest as though he belonged there.

Infants had an uncanny ability to adapt.

Especially ones who'd been passed from one pair of arms to another since taking their first breath.

"No." Sue shifted her weight from foot to foot. "Belle's not married. That's Camden. He's mine, too."

With one last pointed look, Belle moved over to join her mother. Uncle Sam had disappeared. Probably to go check on Stan Wilson himself since the receptionist hadn't yet produced him. Had he really been waiting for his mother to die so he could take over the Carson dynasty?

A dynasty of six.

"She's cute."

Joe's words brought Sue back to the slight chill of the high-ceilinged foyer. She glanced over at Belle again, and then realized Joe was staring at the baby on her back.

"That she is," she said, remembering the changing table that morning. She'd rubbed her face against the baby's belly and Carrie had chortled out loud. The sound, one she'd heard countless times from more than fifteen babies over the past four years, had calmed her. Reminding her that everything would be okay. It always was. If you held on long enough.

"What's her name?"

"Carrie." Chosen by her mother.

"How long have you had her?"

"Since she was twelve hours old. Almost five months, now."

"What happened to her parents?"

"There was no father named. Her mother's young, has no means to care for her."

The room was cold. The day was cold. Not even the memory of Joe's friendship could warm her.

Grandma was gone. For good.

"I thought there was always a waiting list for newborns."

"Her mother won't give her up. She has six months to complete a state-ordered program as part of the process of getting her back."

"How long until she regains custody?"

"Depends on the mother. Could be months. A year or two. Never. In the meantime, because she can't be adopted, I keep the baby."

"You could have her for years?"

"I could." Sue couldn't allow herself to consider the possibility or she'd get too attached. "It's not likely, though. I'm sure her mother will come through. She wants this baby more than anything. In all my years of fostering, I've never had a baby for more than nine months."

And in all the years she'd worked for Joe, he'd never asked her a single question about the kids in her care.

"And you had no problem giving it up after all that time?"

Now he was trespassing. "Having problems is relative," she said. Her last long-term baby had been with her seven months. Dante's mother had loved her son enough to straighten out her life. She'd visited every single day those last couple of months. Handing him over to her had been as much a celebration as it had been a loss.

"There's always another one," she said now, hoping that Dante's mom was still as dedicated to her boy when he was three and four and into everything as she'd been when he was a cuddly little baby.

The revolving door at the front of the foyer turned again, admitting a middle-aged man with a briefcase and a cell phone pressed to his ear who disappeared through one of many identical doors.

Where were her parents?

And then something else dawned on Sue.

"I thought you and your dad's half brother, your uncle Daniel, were your dad's only family." Joe had said so when his grandma Jo had passed away several years before.

"We are."

"Your uncle didn't die, did he?"

"No. He's still here in San Francisco. Still in construction." Though she'd never met Daniel Kane, Sue felt as though she knew him. Joe had idolized him.

Only nine years older, Daniel had been there when Joe was young, and hadn't seemed to mind him tagging along. Adam's and Daniel's mother was Joe's Grandma Jo—the woman who'd raised all three.

Daniel had given Joe his start in the construction business.

"So who passed away?" Sue asked again, staring at the man who'd fathered—and then abandoned—her onetime best friend. "Someone from his dad's side?"

Adam Fraser's father had been a soldier in World War II. He'd made it back from the war only to be killed in a car accident before Adam was even born. But apparently no one from his dad's family had ever tried to see Adam. Or be a part of his life.

"He says he doesn't know what's going on." Joe sounded more bored than anything. "He claims he got a call from some attorney and was told he needed to be here this morning for the reading of a will."

"Surely the guy gave him the name of the deceased."

"Yeah, but he says he doesn't have any idea who the woman is."

"That's odd."

"That's what I thought."

"You don't believe him. You think he knows?"

"How many people get calls out of the blue telling them they're supposedly named in a will of someone they've never met?"

"It happens."

"On TV."

"So what reason could he possibly have for lying?"

"Because he has something to hide?"

"Then why bring you along?"

"How do I know? I barely know the man."

Hard to believe she'd once been privy to Joe's every thought.

"You're here."

"He's my father."

That sounded like the Joe she'd known.

Uncle Sam strode back down the hall toward the foyer just as the revolving door turned again. Sue's parents had arrived. Belle, still cuddling a sleeping Camden, stood with her mother to greet them.

And Sue's cell phone vibrated against her hip. She recognized the number. *Please God,* she prayed silently as she turned from Joe to take the call. *Let my third crib be filled. Not another one emptied...*

Sue barely had time to finish the call—and certainly no time to digest the information—as her parents moved toward her. She forced a smile, keeping her news to herself, trying not to look at the little guy in Belle's arms—a baby she'd cared for, almost exclusively, for five months. She had only six more hours to keep him close to her heart before she had to hand him over. And never see him again.

"I'M SORRY, MR. KRAYNICK. I appreciate your candor and your intentions here. I understand your situation, but unfortunately, I can't give you access to the baby. It does appear, by these documents, that you and the mother's baby could be half brother and sister, but..."

Frustrated beyond belief, Rick already knew what the woman—State Worker Number Four—was going to say. He'd been hearing the same news, in various versions and from various people, for the past three days, which was why that morning he'd finally used the information he'd been given at the cemetery.

Ever since he'd heard from that young girl that his sixteen-year-old sister had had a baby, he'd been unable to think of anything else.

The city's social services network had verified that the infant existed. But they couldn't possibly expose a baby girl to a complete stranger on his word that he was family. It didn't help matters that he'd admitted he'd never even met his sister.

He'd hoped producing his birth certificate, to compare with the one they could get for Christy, would verify their relationship. Would change things.

Turns out birth certificates were pretty easy to duplicate. And alter.

"What about DNA testing?" he asked now, as he faced the middle-aged black woman who at least smiled with compassion, as opposed to state worker numbers two and three. "If I prove I'm her biological uncle, then I can start adoption proceedings, right?"

State Worker Number One, on Saturday morning, had been too new at his job to do anything other than worry about getting things right.

Monday's worker had given Rick nothing but repeated explanations about the way San Francisco's system worked. Yes, the city was the official guardian of the child. The city had custody. But the child's welfare and care were given over to a private organization.

"I'm sorry, sir," Tuesday's worker replied with a slow shake of the head. "We don't have the money to provide DNA testing and—

"I'll pay for it."

"Do you have any idea how far backed up the state's labs are?" she asked. "They've got criminal evidence waiting to be tested. It could take months before you get any results. Certainly weeks."

"And how long will the baby be in foster care?"

The woman scanned the file for a moment. And looked up at him, eyes filled with sympathy. "Probably not long." She didn't elaborate. But Rick had a feeling she knew more than she was saying.

"So how do I get them to hold off doing anything with her? At least until I can prove we're blood related?"

"You could go to court. Petition for a hearing. That might put a stay on an adoption. If you're interested in adopting her, I'm fairly certain they'd give you some time. Would you like to fill out an adoption application?"

"Yes. Please." He didn't ask himself what he was doing. There was no question here. If the orphaned child was a member of his family, she belonged with him. He'd take care of her. Period.

The kind woman handed him a sheaf of papers. "You can start here," she said. "But there's no guarantee of anything. While it's true the state of California always tries to place children with family if at all possible, even if it's proved that you're the child's uncle, it's possible that someone else equally qualified could step forward."

Equally qualified? As in, also blood related?

Was that what the woman had read in the file? Was there someone from the baby's father's side?

"It would help so much if you'd known the baby's mother. If you'd spent time with the child…." *If you'd been around to help your sister when she'd been pregnant and struggling,* Rick figured the lady was thinking. "But walking in cold like this, after the fact, it's hard to believe you've suddenly developed the kind of love it takes to raise a child."

His mother was the reason Rick had never known about Christy. Okay, so he hadn't been in touch in years. He had been in touch since Christy's birth. A couple of times.

His mother. She'd seen the baby. Was that what this woman had just read? That Nancy Kraynick was petitioning for custody of Christy's little girl?

Surely not.

Pray God, not.

"Or if you were her father…"

He'd been a father. A damn good one.

"Our emphasis has to be on the children. On their long-term well-being. And really, the decision at this point isn't even ours. You'd have to contact WeCare Services. They're the organization in charge of Carrie's case."

His fight wasn't with this woman. She'd done more to help him than anyone else in the past four days. She'd just given him the name of the organization that employed Sue Bookman.

Another official contact.

Taking his paperwork, he thanked her and left.

He had to find a way to see the child. Not to convince a court to let him adopt her because he'd seen her, but because he had to see his little sister's baby. Especially if she could be adopted out before he had a chance to petition for her himself. He had to know she was okay.

And to promise her that, somehow, whether she was adopted or not, he would not abandon her. He was not going to take any chances that another life would be lost.

According to Chenille Langston, his sister's fifteen-year-old friend who'd talked to him at the grave site, Christy had loved and wanted this baby enough to "stay off the junk" during her entire pregnancy.

Out in his car, Rick checked his cell phone again, waiting to see if the Bookman woman had called him back. Seeing the empty message box, he dialed his lawyer.

CHAPTER FOUR

WHILE HER FIRST INSTINCT was to grab Camden and run, Sue left the baby in her cousin's arms, falling in beside her parents, behind Belle and Uncle Sam and Aunt Emily, as they all made their way down the hall to the lawyer's office suite. Joe had been in conversation with his father as she'd left.

Probably just as well. Sue and Joe just didn't seem to have that much to say to each other these days.

The room was furnished with expensively upholstered couches for two, four of them, gathered around a central, cherry table laid with eight packets. A ninth chair, a high-backed desk chair, filled one of the corners of the meeting area.

Luke and Jenny were the first to sit. Sam and Emily took the couch next to theirs. That left two couches. One for Belle and Camden? The other for Sue and Carrie?

Belle sat, settling the sleeping baby boy more comfortably against her.

Sue preferred to stand.

Uncle Sam had opened the packet in front of him. Was shifting through papers as though he owned them all.

The papers. And the people in the room, too.

As Belle said, it wasn't as if Grandma's money was a big deal compared to his own bank account. Okay, so the house, built for a pittance back in the '40s, was probably worth a million or more, but then Uncle Sam's house would probably sell for that in California's current market. And other than the house, the most valuable thing Grandma had was the diamond necklace Grandpa had given her when they'd married. It had been his mother's, a gift from his father. And his grandmother's before that.

Sue lost track of how many generations the necklace had been in the family, how many greats it went back, but she loved the story that went with the cherished piece. Had never tired of hearing it.

It had arrived in California with the Dale Carson who'd first come to America from Scotland. The son of itinerant farm workers. He'd fallen in love with the daughter of one of the wealthy gentlemen farmers he'd worked for, but their plans to marry were discovered. And the aggrieved father put an end to their affair. His love had given the young man the only thing of value she had with her—her necklace—and told him to use it for passage to America, where he could at least have the hope of a more promising future.

The young man had made it to America, working his way across the ocean in the bowels of a ship. The necklace, they said, he'd kept hidden away. And years later, in his new land, his new home, he gave it to the woman he married.

The necklace became a symbol. Hard work would get Carsons where they needed to be. They didn't ever have to sell out; if things got tough, they just had to work harder.

As far as jewelry went, the piece was probably extremely valuable.

And Sue didn't give a hoot.

She wanted her grandmother back....

Jenny and Luke held their packets, unopened. Belle picked up hers.

Sue didn't give a damn what any of them read. What any sheets in the packet said.

She didn't need goods.

She needed Grandma Sarah.

Jenny had Luke. Belle had Emily. Sam had Sam.

Sue used to have Sarah.

And...there were two extra packets on the table, in addition to Sue's. What was that about?

The door to the room opened again. Sue recognized Stan. She'd met him once; she'd joined Grandma for lunch a couple of years ago after Sarah had had an appointment with the lawyer. They'd all walked out of this high-rise building together.

She'd have smiled, greeted him, in spite of the heaviness of her heart, except that...Stan wasn't alone. Staring, she tried to make sense of the presence of the two men entering right behind her grandmother's lawyer.

What were Joe and his dad doing there? Looking for someone? An attorney associate, perhaps?

"Good morning, everyone. Good, you're seated. Going over the information." Stan spoke quickly. Too quickly. "Gentlemen, have a seat." He pointed from Joe and his father to the empty couch. "Can I get anyone coffee?"

Joe's father sat. Joe stood behind him. Next to Sue.

"What's going on?" she whispered.

Uncle Sam, his jaw tight, stared suspiciously at the newcomers. "Stan? Is there some mistake here?"

"No, Sam. This is Adam Fraser and his son, Joe. Sarah asked that I contact them to be here this morning."

Sue and Belle exchanged a glance. Luke and Jenny opened their packets. Emily studied the one she'd yet to open. Sue could feel the tension tightening her body and stealing air from the room. If this Adam Fraser guy got anything from Grandma, Uncle Sam was going to cause one hell of a scene.

One of his worst nightmares since Grandpa died was that some freeloader would take advantage of Sarah.

And from what Sue knew of Adam Fraser, he fit the freeloader bill.

Oh, God, please. Enough is enough. No scenes between my uncle and my boss today okay?

And while she was asking, she sent up a quick request for brevity. Her minutes with Camden were ticking away.

Not to mention divvying up Grandma's stuff just seemed so…barbaric. Heartless.

Divvying up her stuff made her seem…gone.

"So—" the lawyer adjusted his gray-and-white-striped tie as he sat, keeping on the gray jacket that perfectly matched his pants "—let's get started, shall we?"

He glanced at Joe and Sue. And at the empty spaces on the couches. "Shall I get a couple more seats?"

"No," Sue and Joe answered simultaneously.

Sue added, "I'm fine. I prefer to stand."

Everyone in the room was looking at her and Joe.

She'd made it through four years of high school as best friends with Joe Fraser without ever having to introduce him to her family. And four days after she did introduce him, he'd showed up in a very private family meeting.

It was like something from *The Twilight Zone*.

"I'm good, too," Joe said. And Sue wondered what he was really thinking behind that cool facade.

She tried to focus on anything but Grandma being gone. And Camden going.

She wondered who Rick Kraynick was and what emergency he had that he thought she could help with.

And she remembered she needed diapers.

Stan had them all open their documents. Adam handed one set back to Joe and one to Sue. Neither bothered opening them. The lawyer started to read— legal stuff about the history of last wills and testaments, about the sound minds of Sarah and Robert as they'd drawn up their bequests. About probate and executors. And then, so calmly Sue almost missed it, he announced that he'd been named as executor of Sarah Carson's will.

No one looked at Sam, except Sue. She stared straight at him, saw the stiffening of his shoulders as he sat upright. Watched the red rise in his face. Obviously, in his perusal of the pages, he'd missed the executor part. Or hadn't yet read that far.

Sue's stomach, filled with nervous tension, threatened to send her to the restroom as she contemplated what else Uncle Sam hadn't yet gotten to in those papers. What else was soon to be disclosed.

"Why are you really here?" Sue whispered to the man standing so stiffly beside her. He had to know. He had to tell her.

Someone had to do something before Uncle Sam exploded.

"I have no idea," Joe whispered back.

Sue's gaze shot to him. His lips were tight, the nerves in his throat pulsing.

"You sound worried."

"With my dad, I never know what to expect."

Yes, but what could abandonment or drinking habits have to do with Grandma Sarah? Unless the man had swindled her grandmother out of her small fortune? But if that were the case, the swindler wouldn't be invited to the unveiling of his sins, would he? Not with the family gathered.

"Now." Stan Wilson cleared his throat, crossing one leg over the other. "Before I get to the actual will, I have a short letter Sarah asked me to read to you."

Sam sat forward, elbows on his knees. He reminded Sue of a cat looking at a fat, cornered mouse. Or an insecure man who was worried that, once again, what he felt was rightfully his was going to be stolen away....

A tiny foot jabbed her in the back, and Sue slowly swayed back and forth, tuning in to the little girl whose weight was a welcome reminder that life existed outside this room. Outside the horrible gray that seemed to color everything since Grandma Sarah had died.

"She left me with some hard news to deliver," Stan continued, his expression serious. He glanced at Adam Fraser, and Sue's stomach tightened right along with the male fist at her side. "I've dealt with a few grieving families so far in my career, but I've never had a situation quite like this. I ask you all to bear with me and forgive me in advance if I don't do this well."

"Just read the damn letter, Stan. We're fine," Sam said, with the authority of one who believed he had the right to speak for everyone.

With her father's condescending tone ringing through the room, Belle shot Sue a glance. Rolled her eyes. And Sue was reminded of a hundred other times she and Belle had commiserated over their dysfunctional family.

Then her eyes landed on Camden and she had to look away. She'd given away fifteen infants. She was used to it. Fine with it. It was a part of the job she accepted. Today, she had no idea how she was going to pull it off.

Stan unfolded a piece of blue stationary, and even from her vantage point, Sue recognized Sarah's distinctive, flowing handwriting.

"'My dearests, it is with a very full heart that I sit down to write to you. First, because I know that by the time you get this, I will be gone from this earth, from you. Sam, Jenny, Emily, Luke, Belle and my sweet Sue, I loved you all so much.'"

Sue's neck ached. Her back ached. Her head started to ache. Tears filled her eyes.

"'And it is with great difficulty that I tell you, in death, what I could not bring myself to tell you in life, with hopes that somehow the truth will serve you well.'"

Frozen, Sue stood there. *Grandma had secrets?* She didn't believe it. Not for a second. Grandma Sarah had been the most perfect individual Sue had ever known. She'd spent her life trying to be even half the woman Grandma was.

"'My husband, Robert Carson, fathered three children. Our son, Sam, and our adopted daughter, Jenny. And Adam Fraser. Adam is Robert's firstborn son by a matter of weeks. Jenny was born later, to the same woman who gave birth to Adam.'"

Sam jumped up. "That's a lie!" His accusing gaze went from the lawyer to Adam Fraser and back, as though the two of them had concocted this scheme.

Adam's reaction, in comparison, was almost nonexistent, though the words he uttered softly were almost the same. "That's impossible."

Joe didn't move at all.

"Oh, my God," Jenny murmured, her mouth open, the papers in her hand trembling as she started to cry.

"What the hell!" Sam's outburst spewed spittle. "You expect me to believe that my father was a cheat who had two bastard children?"

"Sam, sit down," the lawyer ordered. There was no mistaking the underlying warning that while Sam was in his office, he'd either do as Stan said, or be removed.

Sue glanced at Belle, more out of habit than anything

else. Sue felt cold. And hot. And confused. Her mind reeled as she tried to take in the ramifications of what they were hearing.

"Robert was my biological grandfather?" She directed the question to Stan, but in fact just wanted out of this nightmare.

"Yes."

"My father was *really* my father." Jenny's voice was weak, disbelieving.

"It's all a bunch of lies," Sam spat. "Someone put her up to this, blackmailed her to write that. My mother would never have stood for such a thing. She'd never have raised her husband's bastard child."

"Watch yourself," Luke said quietly, with a menace that Sue had never heard from him before. He pulled Jenny closer, looking for Sue at the same time. She met his gaze briefly, and then, when tears threatened again, she turned away.

Someone had to stay rational here. To make sense of this. To get them all out of it.

"Billy Fraser was my father," Adam said, his volume almost rivaling Sam's now. "He died in a car accident just months before I was born."

"Billy Fraser?" Sam asked, his eyes hard as he stared at the man who, if any of this was true, was his half brother. "He was Dad's best friend. They went to high school together. Fought in the war together."

"And he died before Adam was conceived." Stan's words dropped like bombs between them.

"This is all wrong," Sam yelled, as though if he spoke

loudly enough he'd convince them all. "My mother was out of her mind."

"I assure you Sarah was in full faculty and acting of her own accord when she brought this letter to me," Stan said, holding up a folder. "There are other documents here—Jenny's original birth certificate, adoption papers, blood work that was done shortly after Adam was born. If you still aren't convinced, you could have DNA tests done, but I don't think you'll find that necessary after you look at all of this."

"You're telling us my father was unfaithful to my... adoptive mother?" Jenny asked.

"That's preposterous." Sam stood again, moved toward the coffee cart in the far corner of the room, but didn't go so far as to pour himself a cup. "There's no way my father would have done this!" More quietly, he added, "Dad was not a womanizer. He was loyal."

For once, her uncle seemed to be truly at a loss.

"And this man—" Jenny, with tears still on her lashes, glanced to her left "—you...are my brother? My...full brother?"

Adam didn't move. But he stared back. Almost as if by looking at her, there'd be some kind of recognition.

"Wait," Sue said, struggling hard with the emotions swirling around her. And inside her.

Her beloved Sarah had faced the heartache of infidelity? *And* lied to them all? To Jenny? Letting her think she was adopted when, in fact, she was as much a Carson as Sam was?

And what about Adam? How come Robert and Sarah

hadn't adopted him? Why hadn't any of them even known him? Had Robert just turned his back on his firstborn? Then why not on Jenny?

Robert had had an affair with a woman while having a baby with his wife at the same time? And the affair had continued long enough that Jenny was also conceived?

Was nothing sacred?

While Stan turned over Sarah's letter to her children, Sue asked Joe, "Do you believe any of this?"

He looked as stunned as she felt.

"This sounds like another one of my father's fantastic tales," Joe said softly. And then, after glancing toward his dad, said to the room at large, "So we're to believe that *my* father spent his whole life thinking *his* father was dead, when instead the man was alive and well right here in San Francisco?"

"I'm telling you, this is bullshit." Shaking his head, Sam handed his mother's letter back to the lawyer and pinned his half brother with his infamous menacing stare at the same time. "If you think I'm going to stand for this, you're sadly mistaken." Sue wasn't sure if Sam was addressing Stan, Adam or both.

Stan handed the letter to Adam, who sat on the couch, head bent over it as he read.

Sam paced. Belle and Emily spoke quietly, watching him. Luke and Jenny were deep in conversation, Luke rubbing his wife's arm. Sue just wanted to escape.

"Sam, come sit down." Emily's voice was encouraging. Loving.

Sue didn't know how she did it.

"I will not." Sam strode over to her, though, standing behind her. Facing Adam. And Joe and Sue.

Adam, her uncle? And...

And Joe... Camden whimpered. Sue watched as her cousin gently lifted him, crooned to him. And then, with a mind that felt drugged, she offered, "Belle, this means we're cousins by blood."

Finally, a ray of sunshine in the whole crazy mess. She and Belle shared blood!

"What about Daniel?" Joe's voice sounded odd beside her. "If this is true, Jenny's his half sister. Sue his niece."

Daniel. Joe's uncle, nine years older than him. The builder. Sue had another uncle?

"I have another brother?" Wide-eyed, Jenny looked to Adam. And then to Stan.

Sue wanted out. Too many people. Too many emotions. Too much pain.

"My younger brother, Daniel, yes," Adam said, defensive and lost at the same time. "From my mother's second, brief marriage."

Sue listened, one of Carrie's feet in each of her hands, while her heart and mind tried to find each other.

And that's when the truth hit her. In shock she turned and stared at her high school sweetheart. Her boss.

"We're cousins," she said, looking him straight in the eye.

Joe stared back.

And Sue opened her mouth one more time, saying quietly enough that only he could hear, "Thank God we didn't have sex."

CHAPTER FIVE

RICK'S APPOINTMENT with his attorney early Wednesday morning went only moderately better than his meeting with social services the day before. He had a chance, but success was not guaranteed. At least his lawyer was going to file a motion for a hearing and for DNA testing.

Until then, WeCare Services wasn't even going to grant him visitation rights.

And in the meantime, unless and until they got a stay with the court, someone else could get custody of the baby.

Cell phone in hand before he'd even reached his Nitro, Rick punched in the speed dial number he'd programmed the day before.

Maybe she hadn't received his message. Or had lost his number. Maybe she didn't want to talk to him. At this point he didn't much care.

She was to be at every meeting pertaining to Carrie's welfare. To give her opinion. An opinion that, apparently, carried as much or more weight as that of the social worker WeCare had assigned to the case.

"Hello?" She answered before the first ring was complete. She sounded breathless.

Young and breathless.

"Ms. Bookman?"

"Yes. This is Rick Kraynick, right?"

"Yes, ma'am."

"I recognized your number on caller ID," she said, her voice uneven, as though she was still doing whatever had her so breathless to begin with. "I'm sorry I didn't get back with you. I've been a little…distracted."

The words came in disjointed spurts. Was she jogging?

"No problem," he said, when in fact he'd spent the better part of the night before watching his phone—with mounting frustration. "Did I get you at a bad time?"

"No worse than usual," she said, "better than some. So, how can I help?"

God, if only this could be that easy. He'd ask; she'd help. And he could officially pull off the road to hell.

HURRY, PLEASE, Sue silently urged the man on the other end of the line. No matter how vigorously she bobbed, Camden wouldn't go back to sleep. There'd been a mix-up with his paperwork the day before, so she'd had him one more night.

But they'd be here within the hour to take him away from her. One hour. Sixty minutes of which, to Sue, every second counted.

The baby was going to be calm, happy, in a good mood to begin his new life. It was the only way she could rest assured that he'd have a smooth transition.

Or at least any hope of one.

Besides, Carrie was due to wake up, and one thing Sue had discovered over the years was that talking on the phone was a tad difficult with a squalling infant nearby.

"Mr. Kraynick?"

"Yes. Sorry. I was…are you sure there isn't a better time to call? Are you jogging or something?"

"I'm bouncing a baby, Mr. Kraynick. It's what I do."

"Is it Carrie?"

Just that quickly Sue's mood went from self-pitying to defensive. "How do you know Carrie?"

"I'm her uncle, her mother's older brother, and I know you have her."

"I can neither confirm nor deny your allegations, Mr. Kraynick. Please call social services." She rattled off the government number. If he was legitimate, the city would send him to WeCare. And Sonia, Carrie's social worker.

Sue was already walking back to check on Carrie, about to hang up.

"Wait!" The urgency in his voice stopped her. "Please," he said more calmly. "Just hear me out."

He didn't sound like a crackpot. Weary, maybe. Desperate, perhaps. But not nuts.

"How did you find me?"

"A friend of Christy's. Apparently Christy talked about you all the time. She said Christy had visitation rights."

That was true.

Christy had never missed a visit.

And maybe that was why Carrie was so special.

Because Sue had spent a lot of time with the baby's sixteen-year-old mother. Had seen how hard the girl was working to get her baby back. How determined she was.

"Why are you calling?"

"Because you have a say in Carrie's welfare and I'm concerned. I…"

She was invited to all meetings pertaining to the baby's welfare. She gave input for Carrie's sake. And only regarding what she'd seen with her own eyes. Only regarding what she knew, not what she heard.

"I'm sorry I can't help you, Mr. Kraynick. Maybe if you talk to your sister—"

"What do you know about Christy?"

"Uh-uh, Mr. Kraynick," she said softly, laying a sleeping Camden in his crib. Carrie was sound asleep, on her right side, just as Sue had left her. "This conversation is over."

"I grew up in foster care," he said, as though that gave him privilege. Some insider's edge.

"Then you know you shouldn't be calling me."

"I know that, right now, you're my best shot."

"That's where you're wrong. I'm no shot at all."

"My mother was a user," he said out of the blue, reminding her of Joe when he spoke about his father— Sue's uncle now. With seemingly no emotion, as if he didn't care. She wasn't convinced.

Joe, her cousin. Uncle Adam. Uncle Daniel. Grandma lying to her all her life. Grandpa being unfaithful. Her maternal grandmother giving away her mother, but raising two sons and a grandson. Grandma

Sarah's diamond shockingly going to her mother instead of to Uncle Sam.

Even after twenty-four hours Sue still couldn't quiet the cacophony.

Shaking her head, she tuned back in to the conversation at hand. And wondered why it was still taking place. The man should never have called. His life, his mother's life, had nothing to do with her.

Was he some kind of crackpot, after all?

He was still talking.

"The point is," he said, "that while I was in and out of her life growing up, I didn't know her that well. Which is why I was not even aware she'd had another child, that I had a sister, until last week," he continued, almost as though he was reading to her from a storybook.

A sad one. As an infant, Rick Kraynick could have been any number of her babies.

In a quiet moment, with Camden's few things packed, his long, furry snake rattle on top of the bag, ready to hand to him as he was carried out the door, Sue sank down on the couch in her family room.

"All the more reason you should talk to her," she said, though she still wasn't going to get involved. "Christy's very sweet. And frankly, could use your help. She'd probably be overjoyed to know she has a brother, that you care about Carrie...."

"I...you haven't been told yet."

"Told what?"

"Christy's dead."

She couldn't have heard him right.

"What?" Sue covered her face.

"She committed suicide last week. Her funeral was Friday."

No! First Grandma. Now this? What was happening? "I…last week was a bit crazy here…."

Sonia knew that. And since Christy wasn't due for another visit until the following week, her social worker likely figured there'd been no reason to further burden Sue yet.

"I can't believe it. I just saw her…"

"I got a call from the police." He sounded weary. And as confused as she felt. "They were trying to locate next of kin. She had my mom's name on her to notify in case of emergency, but the number was disconnected. That happens a lot with my mother. My mother's last name is the same as mine, and Kraynick isn't common. When they did a search, my number came up and…"

Oh, God. Christy? Dead? She'd been doing so well. Was so excited about getting Carrie back. "She was only sixteen! It doesn't make sense."

"I'm struggling with it all myself."

Sue's mind raced, and her heart felt painful jabs at every thought. A child having a child before she had a chance to grow up. But struggling so hard to make it, anyway. Carrie, an orphan. Grandma gone. Joe, her cousin. Jenny having been lied to by her own father her whole life. Never knowing her mother. Sue, never knowing Grandma Jo. And now this stranger, this man, losing a sister before he ever knew her. A young sister.

"Carrie is my niece," Rick Kraynick said, breaking

the silence. "I intend to adopt her. But right now I need to meet her. To make sure she's okay. To connect with her. Let her get a sense of my presence."

"You'll have to go through social services to arrange that."

"I'm sure you realize that's not as easy as it sounds. I'm a single male who never knew her mother and without enough proof that I'm family. They aren't real eager to give me the time of day. For all intents and purposes, the mother we have in common didn't raise either one of us. All I have going for me is half a set of genes, which has yet to be proven. My lawyer's on it, but it could be weeks before this is sorted out. We're filing for a hearing that will stay any adoption proceedings already in process, but there's no guarantee we'll be granted the hearing. And it's not the state that we have to be concerned with at this point, as I'm sure you're aware. It's WeCare. And their red tape is worse than the state's."

Stacking blocks were strewn around the quilt on the floor, residuals from this morning's after-breakfast, pre-bath playtime. Both Camden and Carrie could roll over now. She'd be sitting up soon.

"I'm sorry, Mr. Kraynick, but—"

"Please," he interrupted before Sue was even sure what she'd been about to tell him. She had guidelines. Her status as a foster mother rested on them. Because the rules were in place to protect the children.

To protect Carrie.

"I have to see her." All coolness, or hint of composure, left the man's voice. "She's a part of the sister I just saw buried."

Sue said nothing.

"Family is not something I can take for granted, Ms. Bookman. I grew up without one. I know how it feels to wonder what's wrong with you, why you weren't wanted enough to have a mother and father who loved you. What it's like to be caught in the system. I survived. My little sister did not. I can't let the same thing happen to her daughter."

"You're already doing what you can. You're applying to adopt her."

Jenny had been adopted. And lied to.

"I've started the paperwork." Frustration seeped from the man's voice on the other end of the line. "But I've been led to believe that someone else is there before me. A possible family member. From what I gleaned from my attorney, the process was already in the works before Christy's death, just in case she didn't meet minimum standards to get Carrie back. If I can't get a stay, the adoption could be granted before I'm able to prove my rights to the child."

Christy hadn't told her about someone applying to adopt her baby.

"And I can't do anything about that."

"I'm not asking you to," Rick said, enunciating clearly. "My sixteen-year-old sister is dead, Ms. Bookman. Right now, I just want to see her daughter while I still know where she's living."

"I'm sorry, Mr. Kraynick. I really am. Get permission from WeCare and I'll happily facilitate a visitation at your convenience. Think about it. If foster parents were able to make these kinds of decisions, they'd be at risk of intimidation from every abusive parent who wanted access to his or her child."

"That's your final word?"

"It has to be. I'm sorry."

Feeling uneasy, Sue hung up.

And wished she could call Grandma.

HE SHOULDN'T BE DOING this. He was assistant superintendent of a fairly large school district. Had ethical and moral standards to uphold. Examples to set.

Yet Rick drove slowly down the street, anyway, searching for the address Chenille Langston had given him at the cemetery. They'd only had one brief conversation but the young girl had told him that Christy had driven her friend by the place many times, when she'd been lonely for her baby. She'd said she wanted Chenille to know where Carrie was in case of an emergency. Christie wanted to be sure Carrie was cared for. Loved. But Chenille was only a kid herself. No one listened to her, she'd said. They certainly wouldn't give her a baby.

Chenille's words to Rick at the cemetery had been "It doesn't get any more emergency than this." She'd trusted him to make certain that Christy's baby didn't get lost in the system.

So he was using the statement of a confused young woman as justification for circumventing the system?

Maybe Mark and Darla Samson were right. Maybe he did need to talk to somebody. They'd been after him to do so ever since Hannah died the year before.

Maybe he really was nuts.

Not that his friends had said as much. But he suspected, by the wariness in their eyes, the shared glances when they thought he wasn't looking, that they thought so.

He'd known Mark, and through him, Darla, for years. Had hired him, in fact, to be the high school basketball coach when he'd been principal of Globe High.

Rick stopped the Nitro in front of a large yard with a smallish house set far back on the property, about ten miles south of San Francisco. It was just after four on Wednesday afternoon. The Samsons would absolutely not approve of this visit.

He could hear a baby crying as he approached the front door, and his heart lurched. Carrie? His flesh and blood?

She sounded hungry.

Rick knocked. And then, seeing the button beside the handle, rang the bell.

The crying stopped. Footsteps approached, on what sounded like a wood floor.

Wood floors were drafty. And…

The door opened.

"Oh. You're not Barb."

Rick stood there, taking in the sight before him.

Gorgeous, feminine—untouched by the trappings of accessories—the woman had a pure beauty. And babies. Three of them. One strapped to her front in a baby sack. The other two on either hip.

He wondered which of them was his niece.

He met the woman's dark brown eyes, taking in her impatience, the blond hair pulled back into a ponytail, the T-shirt and jeans and bare feet. "Can I help?" he asked over the crying, motioning to the babies in her arms.

"No," she said. She was bouncing her babies. One of whom, the crying one, needed its nose wiped. *His* nose wiped, if the blue sleeper was anything to go by. "But as you can see, I'm busy, so—"

"I'm Rick Kraynick."

"Goodbye, Mr. Kraynick," she said, backing up enough to be able to close the door.

"Wait! Which one is Carrie? I'm standing here. What would it hurt to point her out to me?"

"If you don't leave this instant, I'm going to call the police."

Obviously his suit and tie and shined shoes had done nothing to reassure her that he was a good guy. He'd left the jacket on, just in case, in spite of the almost seventy degree temperature.

"I'm going." But he couldn't take a step back. Not yet. All three babies were adorable. But one…she reminded him of… "Just tell me which—"

Her foot shot to the door. And just as she was kicking it shut in his face, the crying infant in blue spewed what had to be a full bottle of formula, as though shooting a ball from a cannon. The sour burst hit the face of the baby in the carrier, who promptly started to cry. It covered Ms. Bookman's arm and chest, her floor, her door and Rick's shoulder.

The shooter, once he was done, let out the most piercing wail Rick had ever heard.

He was one sick puppy.

Without further thought, Rick stepped inside the still partially open door. Relieving Ms. Bookman of the boy, he placed the smelly baby against his chest so he could rub his back. Soothe the ache.

Some skills, once learned, never left you.

"Go ahead, tend to them and yourself," he said, loudly enough to be heard over the crying. "There's no cure for colic but patience. And soft pressure on the stomach. I'll follow you so you can keep me and shooter here in your sight at all times."

"I can't—" The baby still in her arms started to cry.

Reaching for his wallet while juggling the messy baby, Rick threw it on the table. "My license is in there," he called out over the noise. "My school ID is as well. And all my credit cards. They're yours while I'm here," he added. "And I can't kidnap Carrie while you've got her…. Go!" he called, sending her what he hoped was a reassuring smile.

With another worried look in his direction, she went. Rick followed, making sure to stay in view at all times.

CHAPTER SIX

IT DIDN'T TAKE SUE LONG to get the babies cleaned up. Or herself, either, once she had the girls settled on a blanket on the floor with several brightly colored toys in their vicinity, encouraging exploration. She'd have liked to change, but they had a stranger in their midst.

Settling for hot soapy water and a couple of baby wipes, she was as good as she was going to get.

Rick Kraynick, in the meantime, standing within sight at all times, managed to get three-month-old Jacob cleaned up and to sleep.

"You're very good at that." Something about his splayed fingers covering the baby's entire back, his forearm supporting Jacob's diapered bottom so tenderly—and competently—made her more aware of the man than she should have been. Than she wanted to be.

She reached for Jacob. And her fingers brushed against the solid warmth of Rick Kraynick's chest, where the baby was nestled.

"I've had some practice."

Jacob didn't stir as she laid him in the newly changed bassinet in the family room.

"You have a family of your own?" she asked, handing Rick a wipe for a spot he'd missed on his shoulder. Why wasn't his wife there with him on his mission of mercy?

"No."

So he was unattached. The fact made him no more attractive. Made no difference to her. Right?

He'd said he'd grown up in foster homes—a great place to get child care experience. His lack of wife, his life, were not her business.

She headed toward the door.

"Sorry about the suit," she said, jittery and anxious to be rid of him. She had to get dinner started. And she didn't need any more complications right now.

He didn't follow her to the door. Instead, Rick Kraynick, baby wipe still in his hand, watched as Carrie rolled over. And over again. To reach the bright yellow rattle that was her favorite. It went straight to her mouth. And Sue wondered, not for the first time, if the little girl was going to teethe early.

She'd rolled over a couple of weeks sooner than Sue had expected, too.

Her visitor's expression—soft and filled with pain, too—called to her, making her nervous.

"Mr. Kraynick, you have to go."

He nodded. "That's her."

He was moved by the baby. And why did she care? This man was a total stranger to her. So why didn't he seem like one?

"I'm not going to—"

"I know—confirm or deny. But you don't need to. That's Carrie."

He was right. But then, he'd had a fifty-fifty chance.

"You need to leave." Please. Before I do something I'm going to regret. Like let you stay.

"She seems to be a happy baby."

"Mr. Kraynick." Barb would be arriving soon to collect the two babies she'd had to leave with Sue when her third had a reaction to this morning's inoculation, running a fever of 104, and had to be taken to the emergency room. "You have no idea which of those babies might or might not be your niece. Now I'm asking you to leave."

"I heard you," he said, still watching the baby.

Sue opened her mouth to threaten to call the police. He was breaking the law, refusing to leave her home. And then she noticed that his eyes were glistening.

And it occurred to her that they'd both buried a family member that week.

"Mr. Kraynick." She hadn't meant to allow any softness in her voice. He really had to go. His presence was causing her to feel things she couldn't afford to feel.

"She...I'm sorry. She looks exactly like...someone I used to know...." His voice faded away.

Just when she was going to lose her battle with herself and allow him to pick up the baby, Rick Kraynick, the oddest man she'd ever met, turned, thanked her for her kindness and walked out of the room. And out of her life.

"I CAN'T STOP THINKING about her."

"Rick, come on, man. What are you doing?" Mark easily dribbled around him and went for the layup. He scored.

Again.

And rebounded his own ball. Holding it against his side, he stopped and stared at Rick. "You aren't seriously considering trying to get her yourself, are you?"

"I'm not just considering it, I'm going to do everything in my power to get her." He'd given up on family. On making a family, or hoping for one. But he was not turning his back on family that already existed. Period. His mother aside. Her he'd written off years ago. "She's my flesh and blood, man. She's my sister's child. And I know I can be a good father to her, give her a happy life. Hannah certainly had no complaints." With a lunge, he stole the ball from the former college all-star point guard, took it out to the three point line and back to the basket for a score. And when Mark rebounded, he played him one on one until he stole the ball a second time.

In the end, the score was even. Rick was no more out of breath than his former employee as they headed into the locker room.

"I wish you'd reconsider this baby thing," Mark said as they sat, a bench apart, untying the shoes that they left in the lockers behind them in between these Friday workouts.

Half an hour had passed since either man had said a word to each other.

"'This baby thing,' as you put it, isn't negotiable," Rick grunted.

"It's ludicrous, man. You're setting yourself up for disappointment."

Disappointment? That would be a step up from the hell that had been his constant companion since he'd lost Hannah the previous fall.

A darkness that had dissipated, for hours at a time, since he'd heard about the orphaned baby living half an hour away from him. He was meant to do this.

"You really think they'll give a baby girl to a single guy? Come on, man, they don't even like to give them to couples who are living together and not married, let alone to a man living alone."

Rick didn't bother to respond. He wasn't just a man. He was Carrie's uncle.

He stripped off his shirt and shorts, dropped them in a pile in front of his locker and strode to the shower.

The two men had just secured their lockers when Mark spoke again.

"It's not fair to her, either, is it?" he asked, his chin jutting as he faced Rick across the bench. "To be a stand-in for what you lost?"

"No one, I repeat, no one, will ever replace Hannah."

"You think I don't know that?" Mark's gaze was filled with an empathy the two men didn't generally share with each other. "You think I don't know that while you might be breathing and moving, you're no longer alive? I watched you dust yourself off back in high school, each time you got moved to another family.

And then again when Sheila took off. You've done it again. You go to work, you rule with your firm but fair hand, but you've got no heart."

"Then you don't need to worry about me using someone else's baby to replace my own, do you?"

"I'm worried that you're going to take a little girl from the chance of a loving, two-parent family, and bring her to a house of grief."

"Then I guess it's a good thing you don't think I'd stand a chance getting her, isn't it?"

"Ah, Rick, come on. This is me. I'm worried about you."

"Yeah." Rick was the first to drop his gaze. "I'm kind of worried about me, too. But everything else aside, man, rest assured, I'm positive this is the right thing for me to do."

Grabbing his keys, he headed for the door.

"Ma, DO NOT LET Uncle Sam make you feel guilty about that necklace." With Carrie on her hip, little newborn William sleeping in his car seat carrier on the floor, and three-month-old Michael napping in a swing, Sue used her free hand to straighten up the family room Saturday morning. Picking up toys. And talking into the Bluetooth her parents had bought her for Christmas the year before.

"That's what your father says, too," Jenny told her, "and I know you're both right. But I've spent a good part of my life wishing Sam and I were closer. Looking for something I could do to show him how much I love him. And…"

"He had no business assuming that Grandma's diamond necklace would go to him."

Michael sighed, but didn't wake up.

"Well, he did, actually," Jenny said.

"We had dinner with your aunt Emily and uncle Sam last night," Luke added. "He's ordered Emily and Belle to have nothing to do with Adam and the rest of the Frasers, and wanted your mother to agree to stay away from him, as well—"

"Which, of course," Jenny interrupted, "I didn't agree to, but it turns out that our dad told him the diamond would be Sam's when both he and mom were gone."

Our dad. Those words took on a whole new world of meaning now that they knew Robert had been Jenny's dad biologically as well as legally.

Her mother seemed to be taking the deceit a whole lot better than Sue was.

"But Grandma wanted you to have it," she said now. "Just don't do anything rash, Ma. Give yourself time to get used to the idea of not having been orphaned. And I'm glad you told him you weren't going to obey him. You need to get to know Uncle Adam."

God, how strange was that? Joe's dad, her uncle?

She hadn't talked to her boss since the day of the will reading. Was kind of afraid to, actually.

She'd thought his adult coolness toward her had been because of her rejection in high school. But if that was the case, all would be well now, right? Maybe she'd rejected him because, on some level, she'd sensed they were related.

"I've been telling her that the necklace was Sarah's to give, not Robert's." Luke jumped in again, his voice as clear as her mother's via their high-tech cellular phone. "From the look on Emily's face, I don't think she and Belle agree with Sam about staying away from Adam, either."

"I'm sure Belle wouldn't," Sue said, and then added, "Take the necklace with you back to Florida. Don't leave it in the lockbox at the bank here."

For all she knew Sam had a key to the lockbox. "Do you have it now?" she asked, as it occurred to her that it might already be too late.

"We do," Luke said. "We got it yesterday afternoon."

The appointment with Stan that they'd asked her to join them for. She'd been accepting delivery of William.

She'd had Michael for two days. He'd settled in nicely. But then, he'd been in another foster home since his birth. He was used to commotion.

William, at three days old, was still just acclimating to the world.

"You have to see it, Sue, honey," Jenny piped up.

Carrie stuck a finger in Sue's mouth. Sue kissed the little tip. And had a mental flash of a man's face—staring with longing at his niece. Why couldn't she just forget the man? "I've seen it, Ma." She forced herself to clear her mind of the man who'd been haunting her. "Every time Grandma wore it."

"It would help to look at it again, hon," Luke said. "Help you accept that your grandma is gone."

"I don't need help." Unless they could find a way to get Grandma back to her.

"Sue, love…" Jenny started.

"We'll bring it when we come for dinner," Luke finished for her.

Smiling at the baby in her arms, finding solace in the innocent stare she received back, Sue said, "Just bring yourselves. You've got a newborn to bathe, Ma."

Babies. If life stayed about the stream of infants in and out of her life, she could control it. Mostly.

"I sure wish you'd put in for vacation," Luke said. "Come back to Florida with us for a few weeks. A change of scenery would do you good. This next little while is going to be really hard for you in particular, sweetie. From the day you were born, Grandma was the one person who seemed to be able to reach you—"

"Okay, you guys, really, I'm fine. Can't we just enjoy our last night together?"

Her parents' return flight to Florida left first thing in the morning.

And they were as desperate to take care of her as she was to be left alone.

IT WAS SATURDAY, with still no word regarding an emergency hearing to put a stay on whatever adoption procedures were pending for Carrie. Tempted to take a hike to the judge's chambers to find out if the guy had even seen the paperwork yet, or signed it, or was going to sign it, Rick got control of himself enough to decide against that particular maneuver. The courthouse was closed on Saturdays, anyway. It didn't help that judges' chambers were off hallways behind locked doors. Unauthorized people were not allowed back there.

How did a guy take care of a situation when he had no idea what was going on? Rick was going quietly crazy.

Which was why, after another basketball game with a couple of strangers hanging out at the court at the park down the street, followed by a jog and a quick run of the vacuum, he dialed the number he'd been told was reconnected. Again.

It actually connected this time.

She picked up on the second ring.

"Ricky?" The voice was needy as always. And filled with hope. As though he was her answer. He'd spent his youth trying to be that answer. She wasn't getting the rest of his life, too. "Is that really you?"

"Yes. It's me. I missed you at Christy's funeral," he said, hearing the sarcasm in his voice even as he told himself to cool it. "Nice of you to show."

"You were there, Ricky? I—I talked to everyone...at the church. How could I have missed you?"

Rick studied the neat rows patterned into his newly vacuumed carpet.

"I was at the cemetery. For the burial." He'd driven to the wrong community church. He'd assumed his sister would be buried in the neighborhood where he'd grown up. Where his mother still lived. Instead, it was at a church across from the funeral home.

"I was there, too...."

"Not to watch your daughter lowered into the ground, you weren't." His words were biting. Filled with things she had no way of knowing about. Things that, in part, had nothing to do with her.

"No…we left. They said we had to. They lower the casket after the family leaves." Her voice broke and Rick tried not to feel a thing. He should be a master at it by now, at least where she was concerned.

"Nice to know I had a sister, Nancy." *Nancy.* What kid called his mother by her first name?

He'd been about eight when he'd first asked the question.

You're my friend, aren't you, Ricky? His mother's eyes had been slits in her face as she'd tried to focus on him.

Yeah. She'd seemed to need a friend. Though he wondered what being a friend to an adult actually entailed.

You see then, all my friends call me Nancy. She'd smiled. And he'd smiled back. And that was what Rick remembered most about that little interlude.

He'd lost a mother that day. But, hey, he'd gained a friend, right?

"I wanted to tell you, Ricky. I wanted Christy to know you. I really did, but…"

The proverbial "but." His archenemy.

"But what?" He asked now, telling himself to be kind. Somehow. For himself, if not for her. He wasn't a mean man. And didn't want to become one.

"I was afraid…."

"Afraid I'd take her from you?"

Her silence was his answer. Both then and now. She wasn't going to tell him he had a niece, either. Some things didn't change.

"I know about Carrie, Nancy." He wasn't going to spare her, but managed to soften his tone, at least. "I need to know what your plans are."

"Oh, Ricky, I was going to tell you. As soon as it's all official."

As soon as he couldn't do anything to stop her?

"I'm going to get her, Ricky. My baby's little girl—" Her voice broke again.

Rick waited. The woman was grieving over her daughter, for chrissake. No one should have to bear that kind of senseless pain.

"I've worked so hard. Ever since we found out a baby was coming." Nancy listed the steps she'd taken. A list he could have recited for her. "Christy's going to be watching me. And I'm going to make her proud, Ricky. And maybe you, too?"

"It's not right, Nancy. You had your chance. Two of them." He was being harsh. But a baby's life was at stake.

"It'll be different this time, Ricky. I promise you."

I promise, my little man, we'll stay together this time. I'm going to make it this time. I'm going to make you proud of me….

Rick grabbed his keys. Cell phone in hand, he headed out to the Nitro. He needed air. Sunshine.

"We'll be a family, Ricky. You, me and Christy's baby. A real family. Just like we always said we wanted."

It was the one thing he and this woman had in common, other than a shared gene pool—their desire to be part of a family.

Putting the Nitro in Reverse, Rick unclenched his jaw enough to speak. "Is it for sure, then? You've been granted custody? Have you heard something official?"

"It's not final yet, but Sonia—she's Carrie's social worker—said that everything looks good. I'm going to do the visitations and there'll be another meeting or two, and then the hearing before the judge. Sonia told me that unless something unexpected comes up, Carrie will be mine long before summer."

"Are you sober?"

"Completely. I haven't used hard in almost three years. Not even when I heard about Christy. I get tested every week. I'm not going to blow this one, Ricky. I promise. Seeing Carrie's birth—I don't know, it did something to me…."

Something birthing her own children hadn't been able to do? Putting the Nitro in Drive, he stepped on the gas.

"Then losing Christy… This is my chance, Ricky. My last chance. I know it with every bone in my body. I have to give this baby everything I couldn't give you. Or Christy."

Like that was ever going to make up for the two lives she'd already harmed? One beyond repair?

"I was at the club last night," Nancy said, her quiet tone not a familiar one. "James said someone was there, looking for me. A man. From his description, it sounded like you. Was it you, Ricky? Were you looking for me?"

"Probably," he said into his cell phone, when it appeared the woman was going to wait until he'd given her what she wanted.

"We are going to be a family this time, son," Nancy said. "I don't blame you for your doubt. And I'm prepared to spend the rest of my life showing you that I mean what I say. I will succeed this time."

If he had a dollar for every time he'd heard those words, for every time he'd believed them, he'd be rich. No happier, but rich.

"When's your court hearing?"

"April tenth."

Three weeks. That didn't give him much time. Stopped at a light, Rick signaled a lane change, and as soon as green appeared, he cut over, making a right and then another one, heading south of town.

"Would you go with me, Ricky? You don't have to vouch for me or anything, but it would mean so much to have you there."

"What time?"

"Ten o'clock. Can you get off work?"

Get off. He was assistant superintendent. Who would he ask? Himself?

He couldn't blame her for not knowing that. For knowing nothing about him. He'd carefully guarded his life to ensure that she didn't.

"I don't know." He gave the only answer he could.

"Wait until you meet her, Ricky. I've only seen her a couple of times, and in pictures. But she's special. An angel. Our angel."

At what cost? Her mother's life?

"Call me if anything changes," he said. "Or if you hear anything else. At all."

"I will." Then she added, "What I did to you, the way I let you down, that's the worst part of my life, Ricky. You know that, right?"

Worse than your daughter's suicide? "It doesn't matter. I made it through, and have a good life." Good being relative. He had a decent job he enjoyed. A nice home. Enough money.

"I'm very very glad you called." He heard the tears in her voice and felt a little sick to his stomach.

"Just keep in touch." He almost choked on the words.

"I will. I love you."

She needed him to tell her he loved her, too. He opened his mouth, but just couldn't say the words.

CHAPTER SEVEN

SHE'D BEEN OFF THE PHONE from her parents less than fifteen minutes, not nearly enough time to deep breathe her way back to calm, when someone knocked. With Carrie on her hip, Sue did a visual check of her sleeping young men and pulled open the door.

Rick Kraynick, looking too good in jeans and a button-up denim shirt, stood there.

"Uh-uh." She shook her head, swinging the door closed again. She was already having enough trouble getting the man out of her thoughts.

"Wait. Please." The hand administering resistance against the solid wood panel wasn't violent. Or particularly pushy. But it was firm. "I need to speak with you."

There was something about him. A sense of vulnerability mixed with toughness that she couldn't ignore.

And she couldn't give in to it, either.

"You know my number."

"In person," he said. "I need to speak with you in person." He swallowed, his eyes beseeching her far more than anything he could say. "Please."

"We've been through this, Mr. Kraynick. Talk to

social services. Or better yet, get yourself into some kind of counseling. You don't seem to be able to take no for an answer."

"I called my mother."

Christy's mother. Carrie's Grandma. Sue didn't want to care. She repositioned the baby, holding her up against her, with Carrie facing back into the house.

"You have to leave now." She wished she felt the conviction behind her words.

With a glance behind her, Sue verified that both boys were still sleeping. Chances were that wouldn't last long. William was eating every two hours.

All night long.

As well as during the day.

And Michael wasn't sleeping through the night yet, either. Or at least, if he was, he'd stopped since his move to a new home. Which meant, since she also used her evenings to do Joe's bookwork, Sue was coming off a night with very little sleep.

"My mother just told me she's adopting Carrie," the man said, a hint of desperation in his voice.

"I can't discuss that with you."

Dressed casually today, he looked no less serious about himself. Or his business. He had no less effect on her. Sue rubbed Carrie's back, bobbing to keep the baby entertained.

To keep her close.

To ignore how drawn she was to this intense man.

"She says Carrie's birth changed her. I guess she

was there for the last couple of months of the pregnancy and was with Christy for the birth."

"And she wants Carrie."

"Yes."

"If she's the junkie you say she is, she'll never get her."

"She got me back enough times. And Christy, too."

"Yes, but…"

"She's older now. She's already got a job, working in a preschool. And she's renting an apartment from a preacher and his wife. And I just found out from my lawyer yesterday that there was a suicide note. In it, Christy said she wanted the baby to go to her mother."

"Which could carry some weight, of course, but a judge could just as easily decide that Christy's suicide meant she was unstable—not fit to be making decisions for her baby." For the baby in Sue's arms. Why was she still talking to him? Anyone else and she'd have shooed him away immediately.

"I'm not willing to take that risk. Carrie might be one in a hundred to you, Ms. Bookman, but she's the only child of my dead sister. She's all the family I have left. And I, apparently, am all the family she has as well—discounting a junkie who's already had two chances at motherhood and failed. I can't just stand back and let the system take its course."

"Did Christy know she had a brother?"

"No. My mother never told her. Just like she didn't tell me about Christy."

Carrie's feet jabbed Sue's stomach. The infant was going to be wanting her lunch soon. And before that, to get down and move around. The little girl was busy developing. She had places to explore, things to learn. Muscles to strengthen.

"Before finding out about Christy, how long had it been since you'd been in contact with your mother?"

"Years."

"Your choice or hers?"

"Mine."

"And yet you want me to believe family means so much to you?"

"My mother… I'd like a chance to discuss this with you. Please."

Carrie grabbed for her ponytail. Missed. Tried again. Rick Kraynick followed the action with his eyes. And grinned. Sue's insides quivered. Pulling the ponytail over her opposite shoulder, Sue reminded herself that she was a foster mother not only because she loved what she did, but because she was truly good at it.

For most people, loving from afar was difficult, especially loving babies. Many foster mothers of infants burned out quickly or petitioned to adopt their charges. Giving them up was too hard.

But Sue could do it. Loving from afar was what she did. The only way she *could* love.

The system needed her.

And she needed it.

"I don't see any point in further discussion," she finally told the man waiting in front of her. And plenty of reason not to further their acquaintance if every expression that crossed his face seemed to be permanently implanted in her memory banks. "There's nothing I can do with any knowledge you give me, except to keep sending you to social services."

"And there's no legal reason why you can't just listen," he persisted. "You're allowed to have guests in your home. I'd like to come in as your guest. I won't touch the baby. I'll be here only to speak with you."

"On her behalf."

"As one person involved in the foster system to another who grew up in the system. Period. Just talk. Can you give me that much?"

Leaning back, the baby in her arms put her hands on each side of Sue's chin, her big round eyes focusing somewhere around Sue's mouth. As though she could understand that the answer was important. Sue didn't want to help Rick, but he was asking her for something she wanted as well. Information about Carrie. And for Carrie's sake, she really wanted to know what he had to say.

"I don't feel good about this."

The man was entirely too…everything.

"But you'll listen?"

"You have twenty minutes."

Stepping back, Sue knew she was making a mistake.

"MY MOTHER IS A DANGEROUS woman." Rick came right to the point as soon as he sat down on one end of the couch in Sue Bookman's home. Pulling a blanket from the changing table shelf, Sue laid Carrie on the floor several feet from two other babies—both sleeping—and then joined her there. Setting herself up as a human barrier between him and his niece.

Carrie's temporary mother was a definite distraction, he'd give her that. The woman wore baby barf as easily as other women wore silk scarves. That alone impressed him.

"How is she dangerous?" Sue looked him straight in the eye.

"She's intelligent, keeps herself attractive, and, most dangerous of all, she knows how to pretend that she cares."

"I'm not getting the danger element."

"She's a fake, Ms. Bookman. A lie."

"Oh, for God's sake, call me Sue."

He couldn't be distracted. There was no place in his life for an attractive woman. Not now. And probably not ever again. Not a nice woman like Sue Bookman. She had to be nice to be approved for the responsibility of caring for needy babies.

"Aside from the fact that my mother doesn't know the meaning of love, other than wanting it for herself, she's dangerous because she doesn't look, speak or act like what she is."

"And what, exactly, is she?"

"A drug addict. Her parents died when she was a teenager, leaving her with nothing. She ran away from her foster home and got into drugs as a way to make money, at first. At least that's how she tells it. She was a good front for the dealers on the streets. No one suspected her."

He was saying more than he'd meant to. Sue Bookman was easy to talk to. "She had me when she was seventeen," he continued. "I don't think even she knows who my father is."

Rick focused on his hostess, but was still aware every second of the baby lying on the floor with his blood in her veins, could see her out of the corner of his eye. Carrie was on her back. Staring at him.

"And there followed eighteen years of chaos," Rick said. "When she was sober, my mother looked like a candidate for mother of the year. She was funny and attentive in public. She was in all the right places at the right times. Showed an interest in my days, in my little happenings."

"You loved her."

What kid didn't love his mother?

"I learned very quickly not to believe in her," he countered. "Because she never stayed sober long. I don't know, maybe the memories were too strong for her to fight, to avoid or get away from. I've wasted too much of my life trying to justify why she did what she did."

"People are complicated."

Hannah hadn't been.

"Life shouldn't be that complicated. Not for kids. As soon as I'd get settled in a new school or apartment, or both, I'd come home to find someone from child protective services waiting for me, to take me to yet another foster home."

"I'm sorry."

He didn't want her pity. Or her compassion. Not for himself. Not unless it had to do with helping him get Carrie.

"I was lucky. Every single home I was placed in provided a loving environment, a chance to be a kid. Problem was, I didn't get to stay in any of them. My mother wouldn't give me up. And it didn't seem to matter how many times she faltered, she still managed to convince the state that she would get better. And that I was better off with her—my real mother."

"She'd get well, you'd go home and then she'd use again."

"Right."

"You think she did the same thing with Christy?"

"I know she did."

"And you think she'll do the same thing with Carrie."

With his gaze steady, and implacable, he faced her. "Don't you?"

"I've never met the woman. How could I possibly know…."

Sue's hand had found Carrie's foot, her fingers caressing the skin just above the baby's ankle. The unconscious response of a mother?

"You're a professional," Rick said. He wasn't sure what he expected her to do, but he knew that he needed her. Carrie needed her. "You hear the stories. And have to be familiar enough with the statistics to at least have an opinion."

"But it's not a professional one and…"

Carrie rolled, her downy curls flattening and springing back as she moved. And Sue Bookman caressed the baby's cheek. Rubbed a hand over the top of her head.

"Do you want Carrie going to my mother?" Rick asked.

"Come on, pumpkin, it's time for you to eat," Sue said, pulling the baby into her arms as she stood.

"I still have five minutes."

"Do you have more to say?"

Rick didn't stand. He wasn't ready to leave. This woman. This home. And he hadn't done what he'd come to do. "Do you want her going to my mother?"

"I take good care of my children," Sue said, standing there with his niece cuddled securely in her arms. "And when they leave here, I have to let them go. I don't think beyond that. If I worried about the future of every baby I care for, if I analyzed the statistics on happy placements, I'd lose my sanity."

"But you have input before they go. You can influence where they go."

Spinning around, she crossed the room, rewinding the swing. Checking on the baby still asleep in the carrier. And then she turned back to look at him.

"Your time's up."

Rick stood. Pissing her off wasn't going to help anything. "My mother told me today that scheduled visitations here will be a part of her adoption process."

Sue Bookman didn't say anything. Her expression didn't change, not in any perceptible way. But Rick knew he had her full attention.

She was a mama bear protecting her cubs. The quintessential mother. The kind of woman he'd fall for.

"I wanted you to know who she really is so she doesn't fool you, too," he said quietly. And at her continued silence, he added, "You'll be giving reports to the committee and they'll listen to you—"

"Get out, Mr. Kraynick."

He did.

CHAPTER EIGHT

She thought about Rick Kraynick all through dinner with her parents—in spite of repeated remonstrations to herself to get the man out of her system. Carrie's Uncle Rick, with his compelling combination of determination and vulnerability, would have stolen her heart—back when she'd thought she would marry and have children. Rick Kraynick, with his dark hair and serious eyes, was making her tense.

But that wasn't all of it. As she sat there with her mother, she thought about Rick implying that he wanted her to fudge her reports on his mother, if she was favorably impressed by the woman. He wanted her to lie. To keep Carrie's grandmother permanently out of the girl's life. Like Grandma and Grandpa had lied to her? To everyone? To keep Grandma Jo away from her? Away from Jenny?

And why? The woman had been a wonderful mother to Joe. And by the sounds of things, to Adam and Daniel, too. According to Joe.

Why couldn't Adam have known his father, as well? Maybe if Uncle Adam had grown up with a male influence, he'd have been better equipped to step up and take responsibility when his wife's death left him with a son to raise. And maybe, if Jenny hadn't always felt like she was second best, not quite as much a part of the family as her brother, she'd have been less apt to smother her own daughter....

Why couldn't Sam have been told that Jenny was his half sister? Or Jenny that Robert was her real father? What right did Sarah and Robert and Jo Fraser have to perpetuate lies that affected the lives, the self-concepts, of so many people?

It was like they'd spent their entire lives playing the wrong roles.

And what right did Rick Kraynick have to do the same thing to Carrie—to make her into something she wasn't? To prevent her from being as complete? To understand herself. To know what she came from? It was very clear he intended to keep the little girl from ever knowing her grandmother.

For that matter, was he hoping to keep the truth of Carrie's mother from her, too? Was he just going to pretend that Christy hadn't been a teen addict who'd struggled to get herself clean for the sake of the baby she'd adored?

And why, since he'd behaved inappropriately, did Sue feel guilty for kicking him out?

Yeah, the man had had it rough as a kid. He'd lost a sister he'd never met. He'd suffered. Didn't everyone?

If his mother was as he said, he had valid points.

But he shouldn't be airing them with Sue.

She passed the potatoes when her father asked. Cut her chicken. Pushed food around on her plate.

She'd never met a man she couldn't stop thinking about.

Sue made it through dinner mostly because her parents were happy just being with her. They didn't require scintillating conversation. And because they were grieving together.

And after dinner three babies needed baths and feedings while her folks were there, which left little room for meaningful conversation.

As she washed and dried little limbs, Sue tried not to think about Rick Kraynick. He'd been up-front with her from the beginning about who he was and what he wanted from her. And she'd been rude.

That wasn't her way.

If his adoption petition was considered, he could very well be back as a legitimate visitor. Someone she would watch. Sonia was going to want her opinions. She was going to have to be unbiased. Kind. Looking out strictly for Carrie's best interests...

Her father was on a ladder in the kitchen, changing a bulb that had burned out just that morning, when she and her mother came out of the bedroom with three clean and kicking babies.

"I'd have gotten to that," Sue told him while, with Carrie on her hip, she gathered three bottles to fill with formula.

"Now you don't have to," he said, climbing down. "You've got some condensation on the window in your family room," he continued. "Which means a seal has come loose. It'll need to be replaced at some point."

"Is it a safety issue?"

"No, but eventually it'll cause water damage to the drywall."

Eventually, she'd replace the window.

"And I took care of the drip in the sink in your bathroom. It just needed to be tightened."

"Thanks." She handed a bottle to her mother. And one to her father, who took Michael and sat in the kitchen chair next to his wife's. Sue grabbed Carrie's bottle and joined them.

"I really don't feel good about you being out here all by yourself," Luke said. He and Jenny exchanged "the glance." Sue prepared for another two-against-one onslaught of loving concern.

"Are you seeing anyone?" her mother asked.

"No."

"It's not healthy, Sue, a woman of your age spending every waking moment with other people's babies."

"They're my babies while I have them. And it's my job." One of them.

"You know what your mother's saying." Luke adjusted the nipple in Michael's mouth. "You should be getting out. Having some kind of social life."

Thinking about getting married.

"I'm perfectly happy as things are." She included both her parents in her glance. "Marriage worked great for you guys, but I'm just not interested. I don't want a husband. I don't miss not having a man around. And if

I were to enter a relationship not really wanting it, it would never work."

They'd been through this before. Every single time she saw them.

"This is the twenty-first century, guys," she said softly. "I don't have to have a man to be complete."

"Don't you get lonely, honey?" Jenny asked.

"With this brood? Are you kidding?" Setting down her bottle, she lifted Carrie to her shoulder, gently patting the little girl's back.

Her mother already had William up on her shoulder. Sue breathed a silent sigh of relief as Jenny and Luke exchanged another look. The one that said they'd let the issue of Sue's lifestyle ride for now.

"We brought the necklace for you to see," Luke said half an hour later as the threesome walked down the hall together after having laid the babies in their cribs.

"Dad, really, I've seen it a hundred times."

As they entered the family room, Jenny went for her purse, pulling out the familiar black velvet box.

Sue turned away. "I do not want to see Grandma's necklace."

Grabbing her hand, Jenny pulled her down to the couch. Luke sat on her other side. "Grandma's gone, sweetie," her mom said.

"I know that."

"Your father and I—" Jenny and Luke placed their hands over Sue's "—we know how close you were to her, how badly you must be hurting."

"I'm fine," Sue said, not moving.

"We…oh, honey…" Jenny's eyes filled with tears.

"What your mother is trying to say is that we understand and we're here for you," Luke stated.

"I know that."

"Denial is the first stage of grief," he continued.

Okay. She wasn't denying anything. She just wasn't like them, needing to cling to each other….

"We're worried about you here all alone, with no one to see you through this difficult time."

Sue jumped up. "Ma, Dad…" She stopped. Took a breath. Lessened the intensity of her tone. "Really, I'm going to be all right."

They shared "the glance" again.

"Look, I promise I'll stay in touch. And Belle's here…."

"Just don't underestimate the effect this is having on you." The seriousness of Luke's glance got her attention more than his earlier worry had. "You're too much like me," he said. "You take on more than you should. You think you can handle anything."

What other option was there?

But she knew what her dad was saying. He'd retired early from his banking career because of stress-related high blood pressure. A condition that no longer existed, thank God.

"I'll be careful, Dad. I promise."

One thing she'd learned about herself several years ago, she wasn't Wonder Woman.

DRESSED IN GYM SHORTS and a muscle shirt, the same clothes he'd worn lifting weights in the spare bedroom an hour before, Rick sat in the dark on the settee in his bedroom, looking out over the city from the wall of windows. The house wasn't big. Wasn't opulent. But it had these windows.

And a fenced-in grassy yard that had been perfect for a little girl to play in.

Ten forty-five.

Rick sat, looking for a plan.

It had something to do with the natural, sexy woman he couldn't get out of his mind. But so far, the details wouldn't come to him.

So he sat. He stared.

He hung on.

A move he'd perfected over the past few months.

When his cell rang, it took him a couple of rings to find the damn thing. In the master bath. On the counter. Where he'd left it when he'd stripped out of the jeans he'd worn that day.

He tripped over them as he grabbed the phone.

He recognized the number. Sue Bookman.

"Hello?"

"People change," she said simply.

Back in his bedroom, Rick returned to study the city he loved. Fog and all. "Sue?"

"Yeah. Is it too late? I meant to call earlier, but by the time my folks left, William was up again and a little fussy with his ten o'clock feeding. But I can call back another time—"

"No!" He sat on the edge of the love seat, his arms on his knees. She was calling him at ten o'clock at night when she could have waited until morning if the call were purely professional. Had she been thinking about him as much as he'd been thinking about her? "Now's fine."

"I won't keep you. I was out of line this afternoon and I apologize."

"Out of line how?"

"When I didn't like what you had to say, I was rude. I'm sorry."

"You sound tired."

"It's been a long day." And then, before he could respond, she added, "A long couple of weeks."

Definely not a professional call.

"Anything you want to talk about?"

He barely knew the woman. But asking the question seemed natural.

"Not really." Her chuckle lacked humor. "It's just that sometimes life doesn't make a lot of sense, you know?"

More like most times. "Yeah."

"I found out earlier this week, at the reading of my grandmother's will, that the man I thought was my maternal grandfather by adoption, was actually my biological grandfather."

Rick's heart rate sped up. The conversation had just become personal. Between him and her.

"You lost your grandmother?"

Her pause was telling. "Yes."

"I'm sorry."

"Yeah. Me, too."

The darkness surrounding him was more companion than demon at the moment.

"Were you close to her?"

"Very. You see, the thing is, I don't get close to people. I tend to get cramped. To suffocate if anyone gets too close. Except for my grandmother. I never got that feeling with her. Not once."

"What about your parents?"

"Oh, yeah. It happens with them most of all. I don't know why I'm telling you this."

"Maybe because you need to talk about it and I'm risk free."

"But still…"

"Maybe because I want to hear it."

"You sure about that?"

"Yes." More sure than he'd been about anything in a long time. Except for getting Carrie.

"Why?"

"You really want me to answer that?"

"I asked, didn't I?"

It was like they were dancing. Only they were using words to circle each other. To feel each other out.

Because there was more here than a foster mother and a potential adoptive parent.

You're losing it, Kraynick. You've met her twice.

But he answered her anyway. "My niece aside, you intrigue me. It's been a long since I met a woman I didn't immediately forget two minutes after I left her…. That didn't come out as I meant it to sound."

Rick moaned inwardly. He really had been out of the singles scene a long time.

"Maybe not, but it might be the nicest thing anyone's said to me in quite a while." Her voice dropped. "This isn't going to sway my opinion regarding Carrie."

"I understand."

"I mean that."

"I'm enjoying a conversation with a woman I've met," he said, bemused as he looked out over a city that, recently, had seemed to go on without him. "Not with a foster parent."

"You're sure?"

"Yep."

"Okay then, my mom was adopted," she blurted, before going on to tell him about her mother's relationship with her older brother, the biological son of her adoptive parents. And that wasn't all. There were two uncles involved, too. And a couple of cousins.

"And you guys just found out all of this?"

"Pretty amazing, huh?" Silence hung between them until she said, "Had enough?"

"Not by a long shot."

"What are we doing here?"

"Talking."

"Yeah, but we don't really even know each other and… Strangely enough, this feels…good."

"So talk. This feels…good." He repeated her words back to her.

"It's been a tough couple of weeks all around, huh?"

"That it has."

"It's kind of like we were meant to meet. To talk."

He was glad to hear she thought so, too. "We've been through similar experiences," he said. "Both finding out about family we didn't know we had. It's good to talk to someone who understands."

"Especially since we aren't going to get a chance to have relationships with some of them. Your sister. My biological grandmother. And even some I did spend time with weren't who I thought they were. My whole life I thought my grandfather was this somewhat quiet, very loyal, hardworking family man who adored my grandmother. And then I hear that he was not only unfaithful to her, that he'd had a mistress on the side for years, but that he'd also had babies by her? He had both women pregnant at the same time with his two sons!"

"But they never knew they were half brothers."

"No! We didn't even know this other woman existed, and she was my mom's mother! This woman raised her two sons—the second, younger than my mother, was fathered by the man she eventually married—and a grandson. So why in the hell did she give my mother away?"

"Maybe your grandfather gave her no choice. Maybe it was some kind of deal they made, that one of them raise one of their children while the other raised the other?"

"That stinks. Like kids are assets you're going to split?"

Rick leaned back on the couch, propping his heels on the low table in front of it, more alive than he'd felt in a long time. "Yeah, probably not. You said he was a loving man. There was probably more to it than that. Maybe…

maybe the first pregnancy came so soon after her husband's death she could pass the baby off as his. But your mother would have been obviously illegitimate."

"That wasn't my mom's fault. And certainly no reason not to love her."

"But then you live in a society that wouldn't blink twice at a child born out of wedlock." What an untenable situation. "I can't imagine the rest of Robert's life, as he lived with those choices."

"My grandfather's smile always seemed a little sad. I understand why, now. But I'll say this for him. He was there for us. Always."

"Us. You mentioned a couple of cousins. Are they Sam's kids?"

"Belle is. The other, Joe, is Adam's son."

"So you knew this Belle growing up, but since you never met Adam, you wouldn't have known Joe, which means you have a new cousin to become acquainted with, too."

"No, that's weird, as well. Adam's son, Joe, was my best friend."

Rick frowned. "What?"

"Yeah." Sue paused a long moment. Then she explained about the friend she'd had but never brought home. "The best way I can describe my childhood is cloying," she added, by way of explanation. "My mom's the type who's not content unless she's inside your skin. Maybe because Uncle Sam always made her feel less a part of the family, I don't know. Anyway, she met my father while they were still in high school, and they've been inseparable ever since. They do everything together, especially now since Dad's retired."

Rick was beginning to understand why Sue lived alone. And hoped it wasn't a condition she wanted to maintain forever.

"By the time I met Joe, I was fourteen. We went to the same high school—just like my parents. I'd realized by that point that I was either going to spend my life fighting to get breathing space from my parents, go insane or keep secrets from them. He was my secret. I realize now that part of the secrecy was my way of keeping my distance, even with Joe."

"You guys had no idea you were related."

"Nope."

Rick didn't think he had a right to ask the obvious question. A boy. A girl. Close. Hormones.

"He asked me to go steady when we were seniors."

Rick laid his head back against the cushions, focused on the lights twinkling with abandon in the vast world before him.

"Did you?"

"Yes."

CHAPTER NINE

Sᴜᴇ ʜᴀᴅ ʙᴇᴇɴ ᴡᴀɴᴅᴇʀɪɴɢ around her house, touching things—a cold metal frame on the mantel, a picture of Grandma, the soft baby blankets on the edge of a bassinet. She rinsed the dishes in the kitchen. And picked up the toys left on the floor from her parents' playtime with the kids.

She ended up in her bathroom, the baby monitor on the counter so she could hear if anyone needed her, and closed the door. Lighting a couple of candles, she switched off the lights, turned on the water in the garden tub, poured in bubble bath and started to undress.

All with her cell phone planted firmly at her ear.

"Joe and I went steady that whole year," she told Rick, remembering. Speaking of things she'd never told anyone before. Not even Grandma. Because she could. Because she had a feeling he'd understand. Because, as he'd said, he was risk free.

Her blouse fell to the floor. Doing things with one hand was no problem for a woman used to living with a baby on her hip as an almost permanent fixture. The hooks on her bra were as easily mastered.

"Did you sleep with him?"

Why the question seemed appropriate, as if Rick Kraynick had a right to such intimacies, Sue couldn't say. She unbuttoned her jeans, stepped out of them.

"Almost." She told him the truth. "But no."

After sliding her panties down her hips, legs and feet, Sue stepped into the soothingly hot water.

"So you think you sensed some kind of familial connection?" Rick's voice sounded low. Sleepy. But not the least bit as if he was falling asleep.

"Maybe. I'd like to think so. I hurt him horribly." She told Rick one of her secrets. She'd hurt too many people.

And wasn't about to add another to her list.

No matter how much real estate Rick was taking up in her thoughts. Incredible, after only meeting this man twice.

"Was he at the reading of the will, too? This Joe?"

"Yeah. I was standing next to him when we found out we were cousins. He's my boss now. I do bookkeeping for him from home. But we haven't been close since high school. He's all locked up inside. I'd hoped that finding out we were family would bring us closer again, but it doesn't seem to have."

"Give him time."

Time. Everything took time. What happened when time wasn't enough? She ran water down her neck, scooping it in her hand to splash over her breasts.

"Are you in the tub?"

Sue stared at her bare toes, sticking up from the bubbles and said nothing.

"I thought I heard the water running."

Her nipples, also showing through the bubbles, were hard. What in the hell was she doing? And why?

"Would it offend you terribly if I said I wish I was there with you?"

It should. Instead, he was turning her on. She'd thought of little else but him since the first time she'd seen him. And these days, people thought nothing of going straight to sex. People, maybe. Not Sue.

"Are you saying it?"

"Are you offended?"

"I'm trying to be."

"Don't try so hard."

"Rick…"

"I know. It's complicated."

This was the oddest…whatever it was…she'd ever encountered. "I'm not offended." But she was scared to death. What was happening to her? Who was this man who'd turned her inside out just by appearing in her life?

"Tell me if there are bubbles in that water with you. And let me imagine what you look like right now. Let me imagine, just for tonight, that I'm there with you…."

SUE DIDN'T ANSWER HER phone Sunday morning any of the three times Rick called. She didn't answer it Sunday afternoon, either. Nor did she respond to the messages he left.

Her parents were gone. She'd said they were flying out early.

So maybe she'd gone to church.

And then out to lunch. And to a family get-together or to the park or out with friends he didn't know about. Maybe there was a foster family group that met once a month.

Or…

By seven o'clock he'd run out of excuses for her. As conscientious as Sue was, she wouldn't have those babies out all day, missing nap times, and then into the night, as well.

Which meant one of two things. Either she was avoiding him or something was wrong.

He couldn't believe, after the incredible phone call they'd shared the night before, that she'd just avoid him. They'd started something. Sue wasn't the type to tease.

A too-familiar fear tightened his chest. He'd rationalized that last time with Hannah, too. Made excuses when his six-year-old hadn't called him immediately when she got out of class, as was their agreement.

Rick tucked his shirttail into his jeans, grabbed his wallet and keys and headed for the door.

Traffic was light—not many people out in the dark on a Sunday night in March—and he was out of town driving south in a matter of minutes. Made it to Sue's before eight.

When he saw the lights on, he briefly considered driving on past.

He had to knock three times before she pulled open the door. She was dressed in jeans and a long-sleeved, red-and-white-striped pullover, her feet bare. As though she'd been home awhile.

"Is everyone okay?" he asked, still on edge with the heightened sense of awareness that tragedy struck without warning.

"Yes." Since her gaze was focused somewhere around his chin, he couldn't tell if she was angry, offended or secretly glad to see him. Rick took it as a good sign that she hadn't shut the door in his face.

"I called."

"I know."

He nodded. Stood there with his hands in his pockets. And thought of her voice, soft and seductive. The sound of water trickling over naked skin…

"Last night was a mistake."

So she *had* been avoiding him. "Why?"

In the doorway, a barrier between him and her home, Sue said, "I…with Carrie…it's not right."

At least she hadn't said she wasn't interested in him.

"I'm not going to be used," she added.

Eyes narrowed, Rick hardly felt the fifty-degree chill. "Regarding Carrie, you mean."

"It fits, doesn't it? I fall for you. I give you what you want—your niece."

"When did you come up with this theory? Before or after you shared your bath with me?"

"After."

Her doubts were understandable. He blamed her for them, anyway.

"How about, I meet my niece's foster mother. She's

different from any woman I've ever met. I want to get to know her. And the more I do, the more she's in my thoughts all day long—"

"Can you honestly tell me those thoughts don't include the fact that I can help you get Carrie?"

"My interest in you doesn't have anything to do with that."

"But you still hope I'll help."

"Of course I do."

"Like I said, last night was a mistake." She started to close the door.

"Wait." Rick shoved his foot between the door and the jamb. "I hope you'll help," he said, "but last night…my interest in you…that has nothing to do with Carrie."

"Uh-huh. And will it still be there if I recommend that your niece be placed with your mother?"

He didn't like the question. "I think so." His answer was instant, and honest.

"But you aren't sure."

"Last night did not happen with any thought in mind of you helping me with Carrie. I was thinking of you. Period."

She glanced down—so did he—and saw her toes curling around the edge of the door frame.

"I don't want a serious relationship," she said when she glanced back up.

She'd said that before. "How about friendship?"

"I'm not going to help you with Carrie. If I think she'd be better off with your mother, I'm going to say so."

"I know."

"And you're okay with that."

"Not really. But I've been forewarned."

"And you still want to be my friend?"

"I still want to explore last night further."

When Sue grimaced, the tension between them escalated. "You're not easy to peg, Rick Kraynick. Or to ignore."

"Neither are you, Ms. Bookman. So at least we have that going for us, huh?"

She leaned back against the doorjamb, her arms crossed over her chest. "What makes you so…difficult?"

"Me? I'm as simple as they come. Boring, even."

Her burst of laughter made him smile. "How does it work when you need time to yourself?" he asked. "With the kids, I mean?"

"Same as any other parent with kids. I call a sitter. One of the other foster mothers and I trade off whenever we can."

"You think she'd be available one afternoon this week?"

"Which one?"

"Any one you'll agree to spend with me."

"Tuesday?"

"Tuesday. You think you can arrange it?"

Sue said she would. And before Rick made it back to his place, she'd already called him on his cell and told him that Tuesday was a go. She was going to meet him in the parking lot at school with her bike.

She talked to him for another hour while he sat in

his underground parking lot, and had him laughing as she told him about embarrassing moments growing up with her dedicated parents. How they'd wear matching shirts with slogans, traipse through the grocery store as a threesome and flip coins in the middle of the aisle over ice cream flavors. And they showed up at lunch on the first day of school—every year until she started high school.

She had him laughing. Out loud.

Damn, that felt good.

HIS BUTT LOOKED EVEN better on a bike seat than it did in tight jeans. The deep tenor of his voice, familiar to her, from their phone conversations, distracted her from the vision. He told her about his climb from teacher to principal to administration in the Livingston school district—the system she'd attended—as they rode up and down streets she'd once walked on a regular basis. Some had changed. Some were exactly the same.

They were on their way to a new bike path he'd told her about. Along the route of an old railroad track, a paved path that stretched for more than twenty miles.

"This feels fabulous." Dressed in black leggings and a matching long-sleeved formfitting tunic, she smiled over at him. "I used to ride all the time, but with the babies, I hardly ever have a chance anymore."

"What do you do for exercise?"

"I used to hike Twin Peaks while Grandma played with the babies. But now that Grandma's gone…"

There it was again. That reminder. Every single

reminder was like finding out again, for the first time, that Grandma had died.

And that she'd lied.

"Sounds like the two of you were close." Rick's green eyes made Sue feel things she'd never felt before…as though he knew her better than anyone else ever had.

Which was ridiculous. Everybody knew how close she was to her grandmother. She was just vulnerable because she was missing Grandma.

"Very," she said, turning her gaze back to the path in front of them, the trees sprouting new spring leaves. And she wanted the ride to last forever.

"They say it gets easier," he said softly.

"That's what I hear."

"I'm not sure they know what they're talking about."

"You sound as though you're speaking from experience, aside from your sister, that is."

"I guess I am."

"Recent experience?" Had he been in love? And she'd died?

Rick's shrug gave Sue the idea she was on the right path. Did he find the subject difficult to talk about?

"How come you never married?" she asked, hoping to draw him out if he wanted to share with her.

Hoping he wanted to share with her.

He pedaled along easily. "She said no."

Sue almost skidded off the path. "You're kidding."

"Nope."

"How long ago was that?"

"Seven years."

"Is she still alive?" Sue asked gently.

"As far as I know."

"Do you ever hear from her?"

"Briefly, six months ago."

So much for the lost love theory.

"And you haven't met anyone since?"

"I wasn't looking."

"Married to the job, huh?" she guessed. He'd climbed the career ladder quickly.

"Maybe. I'm told I work too much."

She was told the same thing. By her parents. Every time she talked to them.

They covered another mile, passing a couple of other bikers and a pair on in-line skates, and Twin Peaks came into view. Sue asked him if he'd ever been up there.

"Of course," he said. "Hasn't everyone who's lived in San Francisco for more than a week?"

She chuckled.

"What's going to happen to your grandma's house?" Rick asked.

Sue stared at him before answering. Who was this man? Where had he come from? And why was he in her life right now? When she was most susceptible?

"Uncle Sam's got it listed already. He and Mom already divvied up most of Grandma's stuff, and movers are putting the things in storage bins."

She'd heard the words. She'd processed facts. Period. Her life had revolved around that house in Twin Peaks. Around her grandparents.

Her life had been a lie.

"That's quick."

"Do you have any idea how much it would have meant to know that we were blood relatives while I was growing up?" she blurted. "Do you have any idea how many times I wished I was as much a grandchild to Grandma and Grandpa as Belle was?" Sue couldn't believe she was saying this.

"You were! Come on, you more than anyone know that adopted kids are as loved, as valued, as important as biological children."

"To the parents, that's true. But just because adults have it all worked out doesn't mean children do. We can explain, and love, but we can't tell a child how to feel. Or an adult, either."

"But you felt loved."

"Yes, and now I feel incredibly betrayed. How could Grandpa never once look his daughter in the eye and tell her he'd fathered her? I just don't get it."

"At least he had her there to love."

Sue pedaled harder as the questions pushed her on. She didn't want to think about these things. Didn't want to talk about them.

But they wouldn't leave her alone.

"Still, it would have helped so much if we'd all known who we were. If Mom was truly adopted, unrelated by blood, then fine. That's who she was. Instead, that's only who she thought she was. And she has another full brother and a half brother…. To know that your parents deliberately kept the knowledge from you…"

"I'm sure they had reasons."

"That doesn't mean they were right. Or that they made the best choices." Sue's thoughts raged on. "That's one of the reasons I think Carrie being placed with your mother might be the best choice," she said before she could think better of it. "As long as your mother adores her, and stays clean—and with her history, the state won't give her two chances with this one—with her Carrie has a chance of growing up with a strong sense of self. And sometimes it's only your sense of self that keeps you holding on...."

Her parents had given her that. And it had kept her alive at a time when she'd rather have been dead. When she'd prayed for death.

"Your mother knew Christy better than anyone," she said, grasping the handlebars tighter. "She knew her likes and dislikes, her mannerisms and idiosyncrasies, how old she was when she took her first steps and what kinds of things made her laugh. She probably knows who Carrie's father is, and she was around for Carrie's birth. She's the only one who can—"

"I disagree."

His voice had changed.

"I know."

And that was why she couldn't start to count on this man's friendship, no matter how much he engaged her. A baby's life wasn't something you could get around.

Or compromise on.

CHAPTER TEN

RICK TOLD HIMSELF to forget the woman pedaling beside him. After the way he'd been raised, he'd always wanted to have a family. A close family. That did everything together.

Sue's goal was to remain single, detached. Alone.

Or so she'd said in more than one of their conversations.

And he knew with every fiber of his being that Carrie belonged with him. Whether Sue Bookman helped him get her or not.

If he got the baby, where would Sue fit into his life?

Where did he want her to fit?

She said something about turning back, and his thoughts skidded to a stop. What was he doing, thinking of this woman in terms of his future? He'd known her little more than a week.

"I will be a good father to Carrie," he said aloud, as much to get himself back on track as anything.

"Rick, you don't even know if you'll get a chance. The court might go through with your mother's adoption of her, regardless."

He had to get the chance. That baby was not going to go to his mother by default. Fate wouldn't be that cruel.

"Being a parent is so much more than changing diapers and giving baths," she said. "It's more than looking after younger kids in a foster home. It's a lifetime commitment."

They'd wheeled past a familiar road about a quarter of a mile back. He'd given it a brief mental acknowledgment and moved past. Now Rick turned back.

Sue followed without another word. Until he signaled the turnoff.

"Where are we going?"

He tried to tell her, but ended up saying, "Humor me."

"Okay."

He slowed, and she matched her pace to his. The road was quiet. And short.

"A cemetery?" she asked. "Are you sure we can ride in here?"

"Positive."

He pedaled slower and slower until he pulled up in front of a headstone and stopped.

"Kraynick," Sue said, reading the stone.

He nodded. Sort of. As always when he came here, he could barely move.

"Christy?" Sue asked softly. And then answered her own question. "It can't be. The ground is too settled."

But the grave site was still new enough that the edges were clearly delineated, the mound of dirt only partially covered with the spindly beginnings of grass.

There was a stone embedded in the ground at the grave's head, and Rick expected her to get off her bike to read it, but she didn't. She stayed with him.

And right now, Rick needed her. Needed her like he'd never needed anyone.

She stood between him and what he had to have. And yet, at the same time, she was part of what he had to have.

"I know exactly what it takes to be a father."

Sue didn't move, her gaze steady on the stone in front of them.

"Her name was Hannah."

"What happened?"

"She died." Stick to the facts, man. They're only facts.

"I'm so sorry." The tenderness in her voice—a woman who was a virtual stranger to him yet didn't feel like a stranger at all—soothed the rawness chaffing a wound that would never go away. "How long ago?"

He'd started this. "Six months."

"Oh, my God. Oh, Rick. I am so sorry." Her eyes widened as she gave him a quick glance. And then her gaze returned to the stone. "How old was she?"

"Six. She'd be seven now."

See, facts aren't that hard. As long as you stick to them.

"Was she sick?" Sue turned on her bike, facing him directly. The look she gave him held a depth he couldn't describe. She spoke without words. Which made no sense.

None of this made sense. Him with someone. Sharing Hannah.

"She was on the playground at school. A teenager high on acid lost control of his new Mustang convertible, drove through the fence and hit her."

Yes, that was what the newspapers said. Mark had told him. The police hadn't been as forthcoming. Rick had tried to read the clippings. Hadn't succeeded yet.

He'd yet to make it through the boxes of cards that had come to the house. Darla had packed them up for him, left them in the spare bedroom. They were there somewhere.

"How awful. I'm... I don't know what to say...."

Rick pedaled on.

The tragedy had nothing to do with them.

The past couldn't be changed.

SHE STILL HAD AN HOUR before Barb's daughter, Lisa, would be expecting her home. An hour before it was time for baths and bed for her three charges.

And she was with a man who'd disappeared into a private hell she couldn't seem to penetrate. It was as though she'd been riding with a stranger, not the man who'd touched her so deeply in such a short space of time.

He lifted her bike into the van, and then loaded his into his SUV before turning back to her, keys in hand.

"I saw where Hannah is buried." Sue said. "Can I see where she lived?" She was pushing. Requesting entrance into his personal space. Maybe it wasn't wise, but it felt right.

Rick studied her, eyes narrowed, then turned away. "You want to follow me?" he asked over his shoulder as he opened the driver's door on his Nitro.

Nodding, Sue got into the van quickly, buckling her belt and turning on the ignition at the same time. She wasn't going to give him time to change his mind.

Looking around Rick's living room ten minutes later, honing in particularly on all of the pictures of Hannah—of him and Hannah—Sue blinked back tears.

His daughter's eyes were green, like her father's. But her hair was darker than his by a couple of shades.

Sue didn't mean to stare, but the little girl had been what child models were made of. Oozing happiness and confidence. She compelled you to look at her.

Glancing up, she saw Rick watching her. His eyes were glistening.

"I can't imagine your loss," she whispered.

"Neither can I. No matter how many months go by."

He'd shown her only this room. The dark brown leather couches, coffee and end tables, home theater system. The room was nice. And there was nothing that spoke of anyone living there—no shoes left by the door, no opened mail or remote control on the table. No briefcase or keys or knickknacks. Nothing but the pictures.

"Can I get you something to eat? I was going to do grilled shrimp and onions."

"Sounds wonderful. But I've only got another forty-five minutes or so. I promised Lisa I'd be back before bath time."

"The shrimp's already marinated," Rick said, heading to the kitchen. Sue followed and fell into place beside him, slicing celery and cutting up broccoli, sharing the space easily. Naturally.

The refrigerator was covered with photos of Hannah and Rick. On bikes. On snowshoes. In swimsuits. There was one where their faces were painted gold and red—San Francisco Giants' colors.

"The pictures, they're all just of the two of you."

"Yeah."

Rick had said he'd never been married. "So you lived alone with her at the time of her accident?"

"We lived alone from the moment I brought her home from the hospital."

Shocked, Sue stared at him. "Her mother died in childbirth?"

"Her mother didn't want her," he said, tipping the pan of shrimp to fill their plates. "Or me."

"What do you mean, she didn't want her?"

Rick brought silverware, napkins and iced tea to the table. Sue followed with their plates.

"I met Sheila shortly after I graduated from college," he said a couple of silent minutes into the meal. Sue had been eating the shrimp. And waiting. "I'd taken a job at Globe High School. As math teacher and basketball coach."

In the district where he was now assistant superintendent.

"Sheila was the varsity cheerleading coach—an after-school, mostly volunteer position. In her day job she was a model."

Sitting there in her bike clothes, sweaty and with her hair in a ponytail, Sue wished she'd had a chance to shower. At least.

Rick's lover had been a model?

"For a boy who'd grown up virtually on his own, never being in one place long enough to form any kind of lasting relationship, having Sheila around took some getting used to. But in a good way. She changed everything for me."

He took a bite of shrimp, his gaze faraway. "She taught me about love. Taught me how to love."

Keeping her eyes on her plate, Sue asked, "How does one teach someone to love? Either you feel the feelings or you don't."

"Love is action, Sheila always said." He paused, and Sue looked up at him, then couldn't look away. "According to her, when you do things for people, you are loving them. When you spoil them, you are loving them in a big way."

The twinge Sue felt was simply because she was hungry. The bike ride and all...

"So did she?" she asked quietly, reminding herself there was no reason to feel jealous. Rick was with her. He'd cooked dinner for her. Pursued her.

And it wasn't like she wanted anything permanent, anyway.

"Did she what?"

"Spoil you?"

"Yeah." He didn't seem that happy about it. "She gave me a foundation. When she got pregnant, I was thrilled. I immediately asked her to marry me. The quicker the better. I couldn't wait to settle down. To raise our family. To be a part of a family."

To have a family of his own.

The story, as it progressed, was harder to listen to than Sue had expected. Obviously this was the woman he'd spoken of earlier. The one who'd left him. There was no reason for her to envy this Sheila woman. The relationship Rick had tried to have with her was not one Sue would ever want.

"I couldn't believe it when she turned me down."

Sue paused, fork halfway to her mouth. "I can't believe it, either."

"Turns out I was just her current adventure. She had no intention of marrying anyone. Of settling down. And even if she did marry eventually, it would be to an adventurer, not a schoolteacher."

"What a bitch." Sue wanted to snatch the words back the second she said them.

Until she saw the slight tilt at the edge of Rick's lips.

"Sheila was a wanderer. A nurturer, but a wanderer. She couldn't help that any more than you and I can help who we are."

Any more than Sue could help the fact that she was a distance runner when it came to relationships. She had to keep her space. And the second someone got too close, she ran. Not much different from a wanderer, Sue thought, chilled.

"She said that if she stayed, if she married me, she'd always be yearning for more. The first few months of her pregnancy, she really struggled with all of it. Trying to fit into the role of wife and mother. She helped me shop for the baby. Picked out furniture and every baby accessory she could find. Made a nursery out of the spare bedroom in the apartment we'd been sharing. But the closer we got to Hannah's birth, the more panicky she became."

Sue chewed, but was having trouble swallowing.

"I hoped that when Hannah was born, the miracle of her birth would convince Sheila that she wanted to stay with us. I counted on there being some kind of motherly instinct that would offset whatever else pulled at her." Rick sat at the table but he wasn't eating. "But I knew, ten minutes after Hannah was here, that Sheila had to go. She hardly looked at her. Didn't want to hold her. At Sheila's request I packed her stuff while she was in the hospital. Her sister came over to pick it up. When Sheila left the hospital, she left alone. And I haven't seen her since."

"Not even when Hannah was killed?"

"Not even then."

"Does she know?"

"I sent a wire to an overseas address I had for her. She called, left a message. She was saddened, hurting for me, but couldn't afford to get to the States. She didn't leave a call-back number."

"And you haven't heard from her since?"

"No."

Sue pushed back her not quite empty plate. Like Jo Fraser, these women had just walked away?

Sue might not want a marriage and children of her own, but if she had a child...

And she'd certainly never turn her back on family. Heck, she put up with Uncle Sam. Family was family.

Even when they let you down. Hurt you. Lied to you…

"I don't get people."

"Yeah, me either. Don't even try anymore. I gave that up when I was about ten."

"So was it hard, raising a little girl on your own?" Sue wanted to know everything about him. Not to commit herself to him. But to know. And that scared the hell out of her.

"It was rough at first. I was twenty-four, in my first job, and learning about feedings and diaper rash all at once. But after those initial few months, it was surprisingly easy. Hannah was a happy baby, a great kid. Those years with her, they were the greatest. Every day, every hour, brought something new and good. Even if it was only sitting there on the couch at night with her head against me as she slept. I was happy. And if I never have another moment like that for the rest of my life, I'll still die knowing I had the best life had to offer."

Sue could feel the strength of his passion.

And could feel the emptiness of her own existence where those happy moments had never been.

CHAPTER ELEVEN

PULLING THE BLACK, low-cut, long-sleeved T-shirt down over her one lacy bra on Thursday night, Sue reminded herself not to be a fool. Her jeans were low-cut, too, leaving a sliver of flat stomach showing. She thought about shoes, but couldn't go that far out of her comfort zone. She stayed barefoot, as usual.

And just before leaving her bedroom, she pulled the elastic band out of her hair, running a brush through the long blond strands to give them some semblance of life.

No makeup. No perfume. With only babies to dress for, it had been so long since she'd bought cosmetics she wasn't sure what she had was even good anymore.

After dinner the night before, Sue had had to hurry home to get the children to bed. But she and Rick had talked on the phone long into the night. Mostly heavy talk. About life. And death. And what it might all mean. They hadn't come up with anything definitive, no answers for the mysteries, but it had felt damn good having someone to talk about them with.

Someone whose thoughts she found fascinating, and similar to hers at the same time.

Before they'd finally hung up she'd invited him over for a couple of hours this evening. After the kids were in bed, so he wouldn't run into Carrie. So Sue wouldn't be playing favorites with him where the little girl was concerned. Yes, she was Carrie's foster mother. She was William's and Michael's foster mother, too. She was also a woman.

Sue checked on the kids one more time, adjusting the crib pad where Carrie's foot had become lodged, and then went to make certain the rest of the house was in order.

Ginger tea was steeping in the kitchen. Not because it was said to enhance sexual desire, but because she loved the stuff.

Where Rick Kraynick was concerned, Sue didn't need any help with desire enhancement.

She fluffed the pillows on the couch, peeked under it for any stray toys she might have missed, and felt between the cushions to make certain she hadn't lost a bottle or pacifier that might inadvertently reveal itself. She was a mother, and proud of it.

But tonight, just for a few hours, she wanted to be a woman.

He knocked precisely at eight—the time she'd told him to, because all three infants would be in their cribs, asleep. Just. Giving her, she hoped, two whole hours.

"Wow. You look…wow." He stared at her as he came inside.

"You're pretty wow yourself," she said, giving his body, molded to perfection in skintight jeans and a three-quarter sleeve baseball jersey, a once-over.

She offered him tea.

Rick followed her to the kitchen. Watched as she took cups and saucers out of the cupboard.

"I...don't want to mislead you," she said, suddenly pulling up short.

He put up a hand. "I know, you aren't going to help me with Carrie."

"I'm not going to hurt you with her, either," she clarified. "But I won't do any favors or pull any strings for you. I won't doctor my report to the committee. I can't, Rick. I'd quit my job first. I'm too black-and-white."

Cups in hand, she led the way to the living room.

"I heard you the first time, Sue, I swear. I'm not going to pretend I don't want or need your help, but I know you aren't going to give it to me." He took his cup. Set it down. Sat himself down on the couch. "Now can you come here? I've been waiting all day to have you next to me."

She wanted to, but...

She turned to the storage unit mounted above her television. "You want to watch a movie?"

"We can."

"What do you want to watch?"

"You."

Sue spun around. And then sat in the middle of the couch. Inches away from him. She only had two hours. No time to be coy. Or have second thoughts and doubts. She had to be close to this man....

"I wasn't referring to Carrie when I said that about misleading you."

Play the Lucky Hearts Game

and get...
2 FREE BOOKS and
2 FREE Mystery GIFTS...
YOURS to KEEP!

Yes! I have scratched off the gold card.
Please send me my **2 FREE BOOKS** and
2 FREE Mystery GIFTS (gifts are worth about $10).
I understand that I am under no obligation to purchase
any books as explained on the back of this card.

Scratch Here!
Then look below to see what your
cards get you....2 Free Books
& 2 Free Mystery Gifts!

We want to make sure we offer you the best service suited to your needs. Please answer the following question:

About how many NEW paperback fiction books have you purchased in the past 3 months?

❑ 0-2   ❑ 3-6   ❑ 7 or more

❑ I prefer the regular-print edition   ❑ I prefer the larger-print edition
336 HDL EZV7   135 HDL EZWV   339 HDL EZWK   139 HDL EZW7

| |
| |

FIRST NAME   LAST NAME

| |

ADDRESS

| |

APT.   CITY

STATE / PROV.   ZIP/POSTAL CODE

Visit us online at
www.ReaderService.com

Twenty-one gets you
2 FREE BOOKS and
2 FREE MYSTERY GIFTS!

Twenty gets you
2 FREE BOOKS!

Nineteen gets you
1 FREE BOOK!

TRY AGAIN!

The Reader Service—Here's how it works:

BUSINESS REPLY MAIL

FIRST-CLASS MAIL   PERMIT NO. 717   BUFFALO, NY

POSTAGE WILL BE PAID BY ADDRESSEE

THE READER SERVICE
PO BOX 1867
BUFFALO NY 14240-9952

NO POSTAGE
NECESSARY
IF MAILED
IN THE
UNITED STATES

"Oh? What then?"

"I'm…this…I like you."

He grinned. "Well, thank you. I like you, too."

"But I'm… It's not going to go any further than… What I mean is…"

She waited for him to fill in the blanks. And to get it right this time. He watched her.

"I can't have a serious relationship."

He leaned back into the cushion, his arm along the back of the couch behind her. "I'm not sure what's hit us here," he said, his gaze steady. "But I'd say it's already serious."

He was right. However…

"What I mean is, it can't go any further than…" What? How did you put boundaries on something you couldn't define? "I don't want to get married."

Face flaming, she realized how that sounded. "Ever. I don't ever want to marry."

"You alluded to that before."

"I mean it, Rick. I can only do this if you understand that we'll never be more than two people living separate lives. I don't want to lead you on. Or someday have to look at you with a ring in your hand and tell you no."

He nodded. "I understand."

He didn't appear fazed. At all. "You're sure?"

"I'm sure I understand that you think you don't ever want to marry, yes."

Eyes narrowed, Sue studied him a couple of minutes longer. He'd received her message. Whether or not he'd accepted it was something else entirely. But not her problem.

Was it?

It was just that the man had been hurt enough. Far too much. And she seemed to eventually hurt people. Her folks. Joe… She wasn't going to think beyond that.

"No one can predict what tomorrow will bring, right?" His soft words whispered across her skin like a breeze in the hot sun. "Isn't that what we concluded last night? That ultimately, nothing is guaranteed?"

His body wasn't moving, but his gaze was pulling her closer. She nodded. Licked her lips.

"I've been curious about something since the first day we met." He just sat there, watching her.

"What?"

"What your lips taste like."

Oh, God. He was making her crazy. Just as he had the night she'd been talking to him in the bath. And every day since, pretty much every time she thought about Rick Kraynick.

He leaned forward, holding her gaze, and eventually Sue leaned in, too.

And when his lips met hers, she moaned with a longing she didn't recognize, in a body she thought she'd known completely.

HE HAD HER SHIRT OFF. With shaking hands, Rick studied the front closure on the piece of black lace that barely concealed an incredibly beautiful pair of breasts. "I have to see them," he said.

Her nod was all the incentive he needed, and with a flick, the lace was gone. Her nipples were hard. Darkened puckers in the middle of creamy white. He didn't trust himself to touch her yet. He'd be done before he'd begun if he didn't slow down.

"I haven't been with a woman in over a year," he admitted. "I'm not usually so lacking in—"

With a finger on his lips, Sue said, "Shh. You're perfect. And it's been longer than a year for me." She lay beside him on the couch, her hand splayed beneath his shirt, fingers buried in the hair on his chest as she toyed with one of his nipples.

A baby's cry cracked through the room and Sue shot up, fumbling for her shirt, pulling it on over her unfastened bra as she hurried down the hall.

Rick's first instinct was to follow her. If Carrie, or any of the babies, was in trouble...

He sat instead, adjusting his jeans around his engorged penis, and waited. Sue tended to her kids every single day. And night. It was her job. If she needed help she'd—

"It was Michael," she said, coming back in. "I'm not sure what it was. Maybe a stomach cramp. He was still sleeping. I rubbed his back for a second, but he seemed fine. I hope he's not getting sick." She was babbling.

She sat down close to Rick, but her bra was fastened.

He got the hint. *Slow down, man.* She'd said it had been a long time since she'd been with anyone. And he didn't want their first time to be a rushed affair on her couch.

"It's gotta be difficult, getting infants like this, mid-stream, with no idea of their history," he said, willing his body to relax. "You don't know if he was colicky when he was born, or if crying out in his sleep is normal for him." Rick paused, and when Sue just stared at him, longing and gratitude in her eyes, he kept talking. "Most parents get a sense of those things from the second a baby is born. Before even. Some are restless in the womb. Some aren't. And with parents, even if they have a houseful of kids, there's at least nine months between babies before they have to acclimate to a new arrival's habits and schedule. You don't have that luxury."

"I get health history and sometimes habits," she said, relaxing her back. He'd been able to put her at ease. Good. "And William was only a day old when I got him."

And Carrie? he wanted to ask. *How old was she when she came here?* He needed to know every single one of the infant's habits. Was she a happy baby, overall? When had she started sleeping through the night? And how old was she the first time she'd turned over? For that matter, where had she been, and did Sue actually see her do it, or just turn around and find her on her back?

Luckily, he managed to keep the questions to himself.

"I don't know how you do it," he said, referring to far more than adjusting to multitudes of babies and schedules. How did she care for these children, experience their "firsts" and then give them away?

Sue shrugged. "After a while you learn to go with the flow. You also learn pretty quickly how to pick up on babies' oral communications. Most of them are much the same. A certain tone means hunger, another means pain…."

Something he wouldn't notice, having raised only one child.

"What I struggle with most is knowing that, for many of them, the fact that they're here with me instead of with the people who created them is going to cause them unrest at some point." Sue shot him a sad grin. "I want life to be perfect. I want every single baby born on this earth to have an idyllic childhood."

Aware of the depths in the woman, depths she seemed determined to keep to herself, Rick took Sue's hand, rubbing his thumb along the smooth skin, saying nothing. There were no guarantees. Life was hard sometimes. Unfair.

"That's part of the reason I can't seem to get past my mom's mother just giving her away."

"From what you've said, I'd say your mom had a great childhood."

"Grandma and Grandpa were wonderful parents. But there was always Sam in the background, making certain she knew she wasn't the real deal. He was. Only him."

"Siblings can be cruel. Fully biological ones, too."

"I'm sure they are. But at least if you're fully biological, you have a sense of self that competes equally. Not everyone gets that, I understand. Sometimes the best chance a child has is to be adopted out to a loving family. But in my mom's case, she could have had it all. She always wondered who her real mother was. She used to tell me she was sure the woman died in childbirth. That if she hadn't, she'd have never given my mom away. And now, to find out that Jo was just a few miles away the entire time she was growing up... It's despicable."

Rick might have said nothing, if Sue had been anyone else. But she had a way of making him engage, good or bad. "I think what she did was remarkable," he said honestly. "Rather than raising your mom alone, making her the second of two children she had to provide for—an illegitimate second, from what you've said, because Adam was thought to be the son of her dead husband—she loved her enough, was selfless enough to give your mom to her father. To be raised as the only daughter of a financially solid family."

"So you think the picture of Mom, Dad and the kids—the money—replaces the sense of being fully aware of who you are, where you came from?"

"Depending on what it was you came from, absolutely. I certainly would have preferred it."

"You say that now, looking back, but you can't know how much of your success today is because deep down, no matter what your mother was or did, she loved you so much she couldn't give you up. You were that special. That important in one person's life. My mom didn't have that, and has to cling to my dad every minute of every day, and try to cling to me, too, to get that sense of security."

"Or maybe she's just an all-in type of person. There's nothing wrong with that as long as your father wants that, too." Rick held Sue's hand, but he'd stopped caressing it. "And I'll tell you something else," he added, speaking for Carrie more than himself. If Sue got nothing else, did nothing else to help him, she had to understand this much. "I am what I am today because of the love and example I received from a couple of the foster families I was lucky enough to live with until my mother would come along and haul me back again."

Even if it put a rift between them, he couldn't let what Sue had to say go unanswered. Not about his mother's love.

He'd played that game too many times.

And lost each and every one of them.

Sue's fingers curled more firmly around his. "You were older, Rick. You knew the score. You already knew your mother loved you. We were talking about babies who wouldn't remember, wouldn't have that sense. I'm just saying that if a child can be safely placed with the person who birthed them, or in Carrie's case, the person closest to who birthed her, it's the best opportunity for inner peace."

He should stop. Squeeze her hand. Kiss her. Or talk to her about California's educational system. "And I can tell you, from firsthand experience, that's just not the case. I did not grow up with a sense of inner peace."

Rather he'd grown up with the bone-deep knowledge that all he really wanted was exactly what his so-called mother hadn't given him—a loving family of his own. A complete family. Where he was a full-fledged member.

"And you think Carrie is going to get a sense of peace from you?" The softness in Sue's voice, the concerned look in her eyes should have warned him.

"I was a good father."

"I don't doubt that for a second. I'd guess you were right up there with father of the year material. But you're still grieving, understandably so, for your own daughter. Carrie deserves to be in someone's heart of her own right, not as a replacement for the child you lost."

What was it with people? "No one could ever replace Hannah." He gave her the same answer he'd given Mark.

Sue dropped his hand. "And no one will ever live up to her, either."

He had to go. Found himself at her front door without any clear memory of getting there.

"Thank you for having me over," he said, feeling like an interloper in someone else's household. A familiar feeling, yet not one he'd experienced anytime in the past fifteen years. Or had ever expected to feel again.

"You're welcome."

He was out the door, heading down the walk, not really sure where he'd go from there.

"Rick?" Sue called out to him.

He turned, but didn't go back. "Yeah?"

"Can we...is this it already? Are we done being friends?"

Rick wanted to nod. And thought of Hannah. Of all he'd already lost. Of all that her death had cost him, and what loving his daughter had taught him. There were no guarantees. And sometimes the hurt was unbearable.

Still, if he had it to do over again, even knowing how it ended, he would do so in a heartbeat.

"No." His answer was definitive. As was his certainty that he still had to go, for now. He'd never use another baby, another person, to replace Hannah. His precious little girl would never be replaced. Not in six months, and not in sixty years.

But that didn't mean he couldn't love and cherish another child.

He headed straight to his Nitro. He was inside, key in the ignition and driving down the street, before he noticed the tears on his cheeks.

Damn them.

Damn them all.

COUSIN JOE HADN'T PHONED. Hadn't returned her calls. But on Friday Sue received a card from him. There were two kids pictured on the front, on a teeter-totter. A boy and a girl. The inside read simply, "Hang in there. Joe."

Boss Joe sent the next week's work by courier with a note, written in Thea's hand, telling Sue that other than payroll, there was no rush. And to call if she needed help with any of it.

The only other men in her world that weekend,

Michael and William, took turns beating up on her with middle-of-the-night cries. And middle-of-the-day cries. All three babies were recovering from the flu. For the past two nights, Sue had kept Carrie in bed with her.

The little girl had had it the worst.

And though the doctor, who'd made a house call, had told Sue not to worry, that everything would be fine, she didn't relax.

Carrie came from a legacy of pain. Sue wanted to see that change in this little girl's generation.

Rick called a couple of times. He'd wanted to see her again, to take her out on his friend's boat for the afternoon, but with the babies sick, she hadn't been able to leave. So they'd talked. About politics—they'd voted for the same candidate in the last election. About their first kisses when they were kids—he'd been ten, stole a kiss on the playground and been made to sit in the corner; she'd been thirteen, in a game of spin the bottle. They'd talked about food—they both loved scallops and hated squash.

And they talked about sex. A lot. A lot of talk about a lot of sex. By the end of the weekend, Sue knew she was going to make love with him. If for no other reason than to get him off her mind. Not that she told him so.

Other than the focus it took to tend to her charges, she couldn't seem to think about anything these days but Rick Kraynick, and being naked with him.

Based on the number of sex-filled conversations they'd had that weekend, he seemed to be suffering from the same mysterious illness. They had it bad.

Throughout that long weekend, they never mentioned Hannah. Or Carrie's future. Or the mother Rick refused to believe in even a little bit.

The man had Sue's sympathy. Her compassion. Her respect. Maybe more. But she hadn't changed her mind about helping him. She couldn't do anything to help Rick Kraynick. And wasn't sure she would even if she could.

She didn't think it was a good idea to place a baby girl with a single man, most particularly one who was still in the early stages of grief.

No matter how well grounded he appeared to be.

William left on Monday. His birth mother, having a change of heart, had signed away her rights, and the agency already had a long list of approved homes waiting for her to do so. He'd been placed immediately.

Which left Sue with only Michael and Carrie in her care. Left her free to meet Belle for a walk along the wharf Wednesday afternoon. A budding journalist, her cousin was in town for a job interview.

Pushing the double stroller through crowds of tourists along the waterfront, Sue had barely seen her cousin before Belle grabbed the handle of the stroller and took over. "Sorry," she said, with a glance at Sue. "Your babies always make me feel better."

"I know. Me, too. So what's up?" Not that she didn't already know. When Belle had that particularly pinched look, it meant only one thing. Her father was on the warpath.

"Dad's trying to appeal the will."

"Good luck with that one."

"I know, but he's insisting he'll spend whatever money necessary to see that it's done."

"Why? It's not like there's any huge fortune."

"He wants the necklace."

"What for? He's suddenly into sentimentality? Would your dad dare sell it?"

"He says it belongs to him. Period. And he wants Adam's share of the money, too."

"That's ridiculous. He doesn't even need the money. He's gained a brother. Why can't he just be happy with that?"

"Dad's ordered both Mom and me to stay away from Uncle Adam. We aren't allowed to try to contact him, or to take any of his calls."

"Has he called, then?" Sue's mother hadn't said anything about it when they'd talked on Sunday.

"No. Have you heard from Joe?"

"Not really. Just a card. How about you?" Joe and Belle had never met before the day they'd discovered they were cousins.

"I called him, left a message, but he didn't phone back."

"Does your father know?"

"Of course not. But I'm not going to obey him, Sue. He's plain wrong. We have an uncle—and a cousin— that are as much family as the rest of us. Heck, more so to you, since Adam's your mom's full brother."

Yeah. Sue and Joe were more closely related than she and Belle were. And all these years Belle had been her only cousin.

"Are you going to try to see Adam?"

"I'd like to invite him to meet us for dinner. If you'll come, that is."

"Just make sure it's either somewhere where I can bring the brood, or give me enough notice to get a sitter. For that matter, you can invite him out to my place if you'd like. Invite Joe, too, if you want."

Maybe if Belle asked him he'd come. But then, he hadn't responded to her calls, either.

Her cousin expertly maneuvered the wide stroller around a group of people stopped in the middle of the walkway. "It's going to piss Dad off royally if he finds out."

"And when have I ever been afraid of your father's wrath?"

"Never." Belle smiled. "You have no idea how many times you've saved my sanity."

"He's mostly bark."

At Belle's silence, Sue frowned. "He's not hitting your mother, is he?"

"Not that I know of." She shook her head. "No, I don't think so. I mean, that would surprise even me. Personally, I think the mental cruelty is worse. It's harder to see. To understand. Or to fix."

Not for the first time, Sue wondered just how badly the scars Belle kept hidden from her youth affected her. She had been talking about her mother, but it was obvious, to Sue at least, that Belle was also referring to herself. As far as she knew, Belle had never been in love. Never been able to trust a man with her heart. She'd lived with a guy for a while. A nice, steady guy who had bored her to tears.

And then she'd been alone.

Just like Sue.

"I'll handle your father if he finds out," she said. "Set something up with Uncle Adam and let me know…."

With a nod, Belle rolled the stroller up to a bench and spent her remaining minutes cooing to both babies. Garnering smiles from them.

And, Sue was glad to see, allowing the little ones to coax smiles from her, too.

A MESSAGE WAS WAITING for Rick when he got to work Wednesday morning. From his attorney. The stay had been granted without a formal hearing.

"Yes!" Rick leapt up. Strode around his desk, returned and punched the replay button to hear the message again. He had to punch it a third time before he heard the rest.

Rick was being considered as a potential adoptive parent for Carrie. He called Welfare immediately,

He'd have to go through extensive investigation, have a medical exam, submit his home to inspection, give proof of child care ability. The list was long. The requirements didn't faze him a bit.

Nor did the number that popped up on his cell phone just after his ten o'clock meeting regarding the following year's teacher contracts. He took the call.

"This is Rick."

"Ricky. I just heard from Sonia at the agency."

"Yeah, she said she'd be calling you." He could have been more civil. Considering his recent victory.

"Sonia said my April hearing date might be moved."

"The court date wasn't for final approval, anyway," he prevaricated. "It was just for placement in your home. It takes at least six months of successful parenting before they'll make it final." All things he'd found out that morning.

"Right. But you know, once I have her home, they aren't going to take her away."

She was right—until she screwed up.

"So it's true, Ricky, what Sonia says about you? You're really going to try to get her yourself?"

"That's right."

"Do you think that's wise? I mean, look at you, Ricky. A thirty-one-year-old man who's never been married. What do you know about raising a child?"

A helluva lot more than she did.

"And what about child care? You'd have to drop her off with strangers every day. With my job at the day care, I can just take her with me."

He'd heard that from Sonia this morning. And from his attorney.

He didn't tell his mother what he'd told them. Mark's wife, Darla, had kept Hannah. She'd agree to keep Carrie. He hoped.

As soon as he informed his friends of his victory.

They were going to worry about him.

But Rick couldn't allow himself to be swayed by doubts. It was time to move forward.

"I'm her grandmother, Ricky. I was there when she was born. You don't even know what her mother looked like—"

"Whose fault was that?"

"Come on, Ricky," she said, a couple of silent seconds after his barb. "Little girls need mothering. Please don't fight this. We can work together, me and you. I'll give you whatever access to her you want. You can check up on me every day. Heck, as far as I'm concerned, we can all live together."

No. Never again. He'd left his mother's house for the last time when he was seventeen. She'd been passed out, half-naked on the floor, in a pool of her own vomit. He'd vowed then that he was never—ever—going to step inside that woman's home again.

"If you're the right one to have the baby, the agency will give her to you. If I am, I'll get her."

If Carrie was going to have the hope of a safe and secure future, he had to get her.

"Christy wanted me to have her."

"Christy didn't know I existed."

"You're mad at me."

"No, I'm not." He'd passed mad about fifteen years ago.

"You still haven't forgiven me. You're doing this to get back at me, but Carrie's the one who's going to be hurt. She needs a mother."

"Listen, I have to go. I'm running late." It was the truth.

"Okay. Just think about the three of us being a family, please...?"

Thank God, he was finally immune to her begging.

"I love you, Ricky."

"I...know."

Squeezing his phone shut, Rick caught a glimpse of the six-slot picture frame on his desk, filled with random shots of Hannah. And wondered for the first time about the secret he'd kept. Had it been fair to Hannah? Not letting her know that there was more than just him in their family?

And fair to his mother? More importantly, to Christy? If Carrie's birth had changed his mother, could Hannah's have made a difference, too? In time to save his little sister?

If he'd told his mother about Hannah, Christy would have known she had an older brother. Right there in town. She would have had another home to run to, instead of hanging out on the streets of downtown San Francisco.

Had keeping his secret cost his baby sister her life?

Not a breath of air moved in his office as he sat there. Voices could be heard, from afar, probably his secretary and the office manager. Their desks were closest to his door.

Hannah had only been six when she'd left him. Still at the age where she thought he was perfect.

The visual flashed again. The playground splayed with metal. A car so twisted it was unrecognizable. And his baby girl, the only victim...

He'd recognized her shoe. Lying there in the grass.

Rick stood, wiped impatiently at tears he'd hoped were dried up and went out to refill his coffee cup.

CHAPTER TWELVE

SUE WAS WAITING for Rick when he left the administrative building Wednesday evening, her van in the slot next to his. She got out as he approached.

He'd called her cell a couple of times that day. Left her a message that he needed to speak with her as soon as possible. He hadn't heard back from her.

She was in black pants instead of her usual jeans. And sandals instead of bare feet. Her hair was down around her shoulders.

No woman should look so beautiful and seem so unaware of it. It was dangerous just putting that right out there to tempt a guy.

He walked up to her and planted his mouth on hers, finding her tongue, tasting her as he had only once before, that night on the couch.

But as he'd thought about doing ever since.

"Have you been out?" he asked when he realized they were in the parking lot of his office, and he couldn't just climb into the back of the van with her.

She hadn't said anything about having an appointment when they'd talked the night before.

She nodded, and indicated the back seat of the van. "We met my cousin in town, yes. I didn't hear your calls come through, and just got your message. They were asleep, so rather than going straight home and waking them, I thought I'd take a chance and stop by. What's up?"

Rick stepped closer for a better look inside. Specifically, at the car seats in the back—and the babies sleeping there. "There are only two of them. You had three."

"William's gone."

He stopped. "Gone?"

"His mother signed away her rights. A family had already been approved for him." He waited for her voice to crack. For her to tear up. Sue just stood there.

He'd known, of course, that Sue's babies came and went.

He'd just never followed through on the thought. Never considered that each time a child was placed, Sue had to lose a car seat.

And a piece of her heart? Because her lack of obvious emotion didn't fool him at all. Not anymore. Sue took her hurts to private places.

"I'm supposed to be getting a set of twins tomorrow, or the next day," she blurted with a cheer that seemed forced. "They're six months old, born with addiction."

She sounded ready to take on the world. And save two more children. What an incredibly special woman she was.

"My request for a stay was granted." He was almost sorry to tell her his news now, because to her it would mean losing another child. One she'd had a long time. "I'm in the running to adopt Carrie."

Sue just stood there with a blank look on her face.

"Say something."

"I...well..."

"I promise you, this is the best thing for her," he said, glancing toward the sleeping infants. In a matter of days he was going to have the right to visit one of them. To hold her and feed her and begin the process of becoming her father. "The system you believe in might work for most people, but it doesn't work where my mother is concerned. I spoke to Sonia today." Carrie's social worker. "She tells me that in the state of California, there's a fairly large percentage of adoptions by singles. Male and female."

"Generally, single male adoptions involve adolescent male children." Sue's tone was bland. Like a professor giving a lecture.

"I'm sorry, Sue."

"Sorry for what?" Hands clasped in front of her now, she looked up at him. Hard to believe this was the same woman who'd kissed him so passionately just moments before.

"You're disappointed. You don't think Carrie belongs with me."

"I didn't say that."

"Not in so many words."

"I just want her to be happy. If you're the best choice for her, then I'm good with that."

"But you don't think I am."

"I haven't met your mother yet, Rick. But Sonia says she's a lovely, caring woman. A changed woman. And if, when I meet her, I think she's the best choice for Carrie, I'm going to tell the committee so."

"Understood."

He'd just have to do what he could to make sure, before that, Sue knew all sides of his mother. Not just the one that brought the house down every time.

He brushed her hair away from her cheek, leaving his hand along her jaw, and stared for a moment at his skin touching hers. "You're honest with me. I'm being honest with you. Let's see where it leads us, okay?"

Rubbing her face against his hand, Sue watched him. And then turned to kiss his palm.

"Come over tonight?" she asked. "Later?"

After the kids were in bed. She wasn't giving him any head start with the niece he'd yet to hold.

And he couldn't be angry with her for standing by her principles.

He couldn't stay away, either.

DRESSED IN NOTHING MORE than thin cotton pants and a red T-shirt, Sue was ready for seduction. She'd invited Rick over and it certainly wasn't for dinner. She'd invited intimacy. She'd been making love to him on the phone night after night.

She was hungry for him.

And scared to death, too.

Standing in her living room, watching for him

through a crack in the curtains, she thought about calling and canceling. She had the best excuses in the world stashed in her spare bedroom.

Babies.

They could always be counted on to need something.

They'd been rescuing her from intimacy for years.

But tonight, though she held her cell in her hand, she wasn't dialing. There was something about Rick Kraynick. She didn't get it.

She didn't do intimacy.

What quiet time she had left after babies and bookwork was spent alone. Always had been. Yet she'd invited him over.

Again.

She answered the door when he knocked. Looked him straight in the eye. Smiled.

"I can't tell you how glad I am to be here." His voice was low. Husky. He smiled back.

Before he could lean in for another one of those devastating kisses, Sue led him into the living room. A place he'd been before. She watched him sit in the same spot on the couch he'd sat the night they kissed. She wanted him there.

Badly.

He was in jeans again. And a button-down blue plaid shirt. He didn't kick off his loafers. Loosen his shirt. Or reach for her. He just put an arm along the back of the couch, watched her stand with a hand on one of the bassinets lined neatly along the wall, and said, "Okay, out with it."

"You make me crazy with feelings and I need… this…but I'm scared." They were way past game playing.

"This? As in us? Being friends?"

"Having sex."

He frowned, but looked more baffled than displeased. "You mean tonight? Because, while I always hope, I certainly don't come over here counting on getting you into bed. Or thinking tonight will be the night."

God, he was so sweet. Why in the hell couldn't she have met the man before she became the person she was? Before she'd gone to college and changed herself forever?

"Not just tonight. I…the intensity between us…it's hard to take." She was tired, that was all. She'd missed William at bath time tonight. And dinner. But that would pass. It always did.

"Hard to take?" Rick sat forward, on the edge of the couch, his arms on his knees. "How? I'm nothing to be afraid of, Sue. What have I done?"

"Invaded my thoughts." Her honesty was going to get her in trouble. She just knew it. But silence, allowing whatever had been building between them to continue growing, would be worse. "I think about you," she continued, all the confusion she felt inside spilling out. "I watch for your car, happy you might appear unexpectedly. I can be in a rotten mood, and you call and suddenly the world is fine."

"I'm going through all the same stuff."

"Well, stop."

"I don't seem to be able to do that."

That got her. "You've tried?"

"Not really."

She wanted him. Now. "I hate not being in control."

"Of me? Or of yourself?"

"Of me. Of my feelings. The situation."

The warm, full look in his eyes flooded her with feeling, until she was drowning in sensations she couldn't identify, analyze or control.

Rick stood and took her hand. She looked up at him. Moved when he tugged her gently forward. And withstood his gaze as he studied her.

She watched his head lower. He was coming closer, and she did nothing to stop him. His mouth covered hers.

Sue thought she whimpered. She knew she soared. God, life had never felt like this. Never so vital. So... intense.

And then he pulled her down to the couch.

"Tell me why you're so afraid of losing control."

Uh-uh. That kind of stuff led to secrets. Telling them. "You never know what might happen."

"Oh, I think in this situation what's going to happen is pretty clear."

His arm around her, he ran his fingers through her hair. She shivered. And craved more.

"You've had a lover, right?" The question wasn't judgmental, one way or the other. Maybe that was why it wasn't threatening, either.

"Yeah. A couple."

"And?"

"Nothing."

"What does that mean?"

"I felt nothing." Just like she was scared to death she was going to feel if he ever touched her down below. She was going to turn off. Back away. Emotionally first, then physically.

"You said it had been longer than a year for you. How much longer?"

Wetting parched lips, she said, "A lot."

His hand moved from her hair to her shoulder. Beneath her T-shirt. He'd know by now that she wasn't wearing a bra. If he hadn't already figured that out.

"Was someone…rough with you? Is that what you're trying to tell me?"

"No. It wasn't anything like that. I can't…don't…"

"Maybe you just weren't with the right man."

No man was the right man. When anyone got too close, she dried up.

"I want to make love to you, Sue. Now."

"Rick…" That was it. She couldn't come up with anything more.

"I like it when you say my name."

She liked him. Too much.

"I wasn't kidding, Rick. I don't do intimacy well. I can't come through for you."

"Why don't you let me decide what you do for me?"

Shaking her head, Sue told herself to move away from him. She had to get away. She wasn't arguing the point; she just wasn't moving yet, either.

"I'll hurt you," she said.

"How can you if I have no expectations?"

She thought about that.

"You've been honest with me from the beginning, Sue. About everything. You and I don't agree about Carrie's future. You've been very clear about your need to remain unattached. And I believe you."

"Then…"

"I still want to make love with you."

"Why?"

"This is the first completely good feeling I've known in months. I don't just want to have sex. I'm consumed by this need to make love to you. I want your mind connected to mine, your heart and soul. And your body. Just for moments, if that's all you have. I've never felt anything like this and I damn sure don't want to die never knowing where it goes."

She wanted him, too. For the moment.

"If I say stop, you stop," she told him. "No matter what."

"That's a given."

"And when I disappear, you don't get mad."

"Of course not. It's mutual all the way or it doesn't happen. Period."

"And no expectations."

"None."

Her body was so on fire she could hardly hold on to rational thought. "I'm not going to change my mind about Carrie," she told him.

"I know that."

"I can't do what you want."

"Oh, that's where you're wrong. I'm aching and miserable and you are exactly what I need to get to heaven." Rick leaned forward, pushing her back along the couch, coming down to lie on top of her. With one of his legs between hers, he moved along her thigh. Back and forth. Up and down. Rubbing his thigh against her as he did so.

And his penis against her leg.

He was rock hard. And felt so good. So right. So...hers.

"I give up," she whispered, licking her lips and then his. "Make love to me, Rick, before I lose what sanity I have left."

RICK TOOK HIS TIME. He should be racing to the finish, unable to wait after so long. Hornier than horny from their nights of sex talk. Instead, he savored every second with her. Being with Sue wasn't about orgasm. It was about connecting with her. Learning her better than anyone ever had before.

He touched her through her clothes, first. His body against hers. And then with his hands. All over her. He wanted to know what that space on the inside of her elbow felt like. The joint between her torso and her thighs. He touched her behind the knees and at the base of her throat. He ran his hands over her bottom. And again.

She let him. And his penis, already hard, stiffened more.

Her breasts were soft. Full. He could hardly believe he had them in his hands. Her nipples quickly became buds beneath his fingers. He stimulated them until she was rocking beside him. Pushing up against him.

He had to pull his hips back before he spilled himself.

He didn't even have her clothes off yet.

Pushing her hand between them, Sue tugged at the strap of his belt, releasing it. His jeans came undone just as quickly.

And he could breathe again. Sort of.

"You okay?" he asked, her fingers on his pants.

"Umm-hmm." With her lips against his ear, then his mouth, she rolled, and he let her, helping her up on top of him.

He didn't help much when, over the next several minutes, she took her time undressing the rest of him. He watched, though.

Oh, God, he watched.

As she unbuttoned his shirt. Ran her fingers through the hair on his chest. And down to his navel. As she teased his nipples. And brushed against the hair she'd exposed at his groin.

She sat astride him and slowly lifted up her top. Very slowly.

"You're asking for trouble," he half growled, half groaned.

"Yeah. I thought so." But she didn't change her course.

And that's when Rick stopped being a spectator. As soon as her breasts were out there for him to see, he touched them. Pulled her down to him. Kissed them.

Kissed as much of her as he could reach. And then he rolled her over onto her back, lying beside her as he finished undressing her and spread her legs. Caressed her. Learning from her expression where and how she best liked his touch.

How to drive her wild.

And then, sliding in between those spread legs, Rick tested her body. She was slick and eager and he buried himself inside her. Again and again. Finding something he didn't know existed. In himself. In her. Between the two of them.

Bringing them to a simultaneous orgasm that catapulted him back into the land of the living.

"Don't ever let it be said that you can't," he said, breathless, as he sank against the couch. "'Cause I gotta tell you, lady, you can. Oh, God, you can."

"That was…a new thing." Her voice sounded strangled.

He'd done it to her, too. Good.

CHAPTER THIRTEEN

"MOM. ABSOLUTELY DO NOT give Uncle Sam that necklace." Sue was lying in bed Friday morning, still in her pajamas at nine-thirty.

"He's going to contest the will, sweetie."

Sue and Michael had been up several times during the night, though the little boy didn't have a fever or any other obvious sign of discomfort.

"I know. And so what? He's not going to win. He's just making an ass of himself." Carrie had slept through the night, as usual, but had been up at six.

"He's my brother, Sue. I love him."

And right now, Michael and Carrie were in her king-size bed with her. Sound asleep. The peace was nice.

"I know," she said. "But that doesn't make him right."

"That's what I've been telling her," Luke interjected. They had her on speakerphone, as always.

"It's not so much a matter of right and wrong," Jenny argued. "The whole situation's a mess. We're all different than we thought we were. And Sam's identity, his belief that he was the head of the family—I don't know.

It meant a lot to him. He idolized our dad. And now what has he got to idolize? One man, loving two women, it's just…how do you make that right?"

"It's not right that Uncle Sam is pressuring you." Sue couldn't help her mother as much as she should. Couldn't be her strength. Mostly because she was struggling too much herself.

"Maybe not, but he's not been treated fairly, either."

"Your mother has a point here, Sue."

She adjusted the pillow behind her, pulling another over, sitting more upright.

"Think about it," Jenny continued, sounding almost defensive. On her brother's behalf. "He was raised as our dad's only namesake, his only son, and with Dad's constant guidance, spent his entire life trying to live up to Dad's expectations. Only to find out, and not from his father, that Dad has another son, an older son. And a grandson, too. And he was told by Dad that as a symbol of the family legacy, he'd have the Carson diamond."

"He was lied to, like the rest of us," Sue said, resting a hand against Carrie's side. Was the baby going to grow up knowing the truth of her heritage? And would she also be loved and adored? Or only cared for?

"He says he wants to give the necklace to Emily—"

"And I think he's playing your mother, Sue," Luke interrupted, with more compassion than accusation. "He said he and your mother were the real Carsons and they had to stick together."

Sue bit back a surge of anger. Her mother had spent

her entire life trying to gain Sam's acceptance. And the bastard knew it.

Belle's father. A man who was misguided, most definitely. The bastard who was the only one in the family who wasn't truly a bastard in the literal sense.

"Mom, please. Just hang on to the necklace."

"He says he'll will it to you," Jenny said.

"Grandma wanted you to have it. Uncle Sam might have been her only birth child, but she saw him for what he was. And she didn't want him to have it, Mom. There's obviously a reason for that. Please trust her judgment and hang on to it."

Her judgment? Grandma had lied to them.

"I think your grandmother was afraid Uncle Sam would sell the necklace," Luke said.

"I don't think he would," Jenny insisted.

"I do." Sue had no doubt about it. Sentimental value meant nothing to Sam. And the diamond was worth more money than Sue wanted to think about. "But I don't think that's why she wanted Mom to have it. I think Grandma was telling Mom something about being a Carson. Reinforcing that she truly loved mom as a daughter. Just make sure it's safe, Ma," she added. "And hold on to it. Let's deal with having Uncle Adam and Joe in our lives, first."

"Right," Luke said. "And by the way, Sue—"

"Yes, by the way," Jenny piped, the renewed energy in her voice alerting Sue that her mother was coming after her again. "You knew your cousin Joe *before* Stan's announcement. Brought him to the funeral. What was that about?"

It was time for a baby to wake up. To cry and pull her away. She considered lying. And heard Grandma's voice, from almost twenty years ago, telling her that she didn't have to be who her parents wanted her to be—that she was perfect being just who she was—but that she owed it to them and to herself to always be honest with them.

And with few exceptions, she always had been. She kept secrets, but she didn't lie.

Funny that the woman who'd taught her that was the biggest liar of all.

"I was friends with him in high school." She finally gave them the version of the truth she could. "We ran into each other again a few years ago, when I was looking for clients. He's the builder I do books for."

"In high school?" Jenny sounded bewildered.

"We never heard of a Joe Fraser," Luke added, a second behind his wife. "How could you have known him?"

Ah, guys... "I just didn't mention him, that's all."

"You were just acquaintances, then," Jenny said.

"More than that. He was in the group with Shelly and Brian and the rest."

"He was the one!" Jenny sounded as though a great mystery had been solved.

Carrie stirred, but didn't wake up. Her chubby cheeks with their bright pink spots scrunched and relaxed.

"What one?" Sue asked.

"The boy you didn't want us to know about."

Shaking her head, having a hard time believing this bizarre conversation, she asked, "How'd you find out there was a boy?"

"A mom knows these things," Jenny said.

And Luke added, "The way you went off into your own thoughts and then grinned was a pretty good give-away, too."

"I can't believe this!"

"So why didn't you tell us about him, Sue?" Jenny's question held no bitterness.

Because he never wanted to come to the house. Sue was tempted to offer the easy answer. But not the truthful one.

Just like Grandma.

"Joe was my attempt to be my own person," she finally said softly, praying they'd understand. That what she said didn't hurt them more than lying to them would have. "I was young and…"

"And you had to have your own life," Luke said. "You were going to leave our nest soon and you had to find out if you could make it without us."

Sue sank back into the pillows. "I can't believe you guessed I liked someone, and didn't ask about him."

"You were making a bid for independence. We had to respect that."

Were these her parents? In her life? Because this wasn't how she'd seen it at all. Wow.

"I don't have any idea what to say."

"Just tell us that you and Joe…you didn't—" Jenny broke off, and for once Luke didn't jump in.

"No!" Sue said quickly. And then, glancing at the babies asleep beside her, lowered her voice. "No. We held hands. That's all."

"So you and Adam's son were close friends," Jenny

mused. "I'm glad that you at least grew up knowing one of your relatives."

Unlike Jenny. Who hadn't known Joe, or Adam or her own mother.

"Yeah," Sue said. "Me, too."

"And he's a good guy?"

"The best, though he's a lot more reserved now then he was in school."

"Do you think he'd help us get his dad into the family? Adam's answered a couple of my calls, but always has to go right away. He's my full brother," Jenny said. "I really really want to get to know him."

Full brother. The facts hit Sue again. And still seemed so foreign. So impossible. As though she were living someone else's life.

And then something else occurred to her. If her mother developed a relationship with Adam, then maybe she wouldn't need Uncle Sam's acceptance so badly. Maybe she'd find that inner peace that had been missing most of her life.

"I'll see what I can do," she said, making a mental note to call Belle to see how she was doing setting up a dinner with them and the Frasers.

And then she sent up a silent prayer for a softening of Joe's heart. He didn't even like his dad. And wasn't talking much to her, either.

But Sue wasn't one to be daunted.

WHEN SUE CALLED RICK Friday afternoon, telling him she had a problem at home and needed help, he was out of the office as quickly as he could grab his keys, inordinately pleased that she'd called *him*.

That he was the one she'd turned to.

He'd had a school board meeting the night before and had been tied up until almost eleven o'clock, but he'd talked to her as he drove home, and for an hour afterward.

She'd been in bed, and he'd spent a good part of the night wishing he'd been there with her.

And wondering if there would ever come a time when they'd share a bed. Permanently.

Rick didn't want to spend the rest of his life alone. He wanted a wife. A partner.

He wanted a family.

Sue didn't.

He didn't know what to do about that.

But some things were working in his favor. Sonia had called to say that she'd arranged visitation between him and Carrie twice a week, Mondays and Wednesdays from four to five, starting right away.

He was finally going to be able to hold his niece.

Sonia told him something else, as well. His mother's visitation had also been scheduled. Even the idea of it made Rick's blood pressure rise.

If he could count on Sue to protect Carrie's future from an addicted liar…

If he could count on her not to fall under his mother's spell…

If only he could count on her, period.

When she answered the door, Carrie in the pack on her back and an unfamiliar, too skinny baby in her arms,

Sue's hair was falling out of her ponytail, tendrils hanging around her face. There were stains on her blue-and-white-striped, long-sleeved T-shirt. And a blotch on the thigh of her jeans, as well.

He'd have liked to kiss her—long and hard—but there were obviously other matters pressing. "Thank you so much for coming." She added, "Would you mind taking him?" She carefully handed him the blanket-wrapped, sleeping bundle in her arms before the door was even fully closed.

As he took the unknown boy, Rick caught Carrie staring at him. He grinned. And the baby grinned back.

"His brother just threw up all over the living room floor," Sue said, leaving Rick to follow her. "I've been trying since noon to feed the two of them. They both give it back as soon as I get it down them."

"Not uncommon for babies born with addictions," Rick expostulated. "They're often finicky eaters."

From her place on the floor beside a baby that looked identical to the one he had in his arms, Sue glanced up at him.

"They have sleeping disorders, too," he stated. "And tremors."

She turned back to the job at hand, gently cleaning up the baby with baby wipes from the canister by her side. The blanket she and the infant were on was covered with spat-up formula.

With the sleeping brother in the crook of one arm, and a quick caress to Michael's cheek where he sat in a swing, Rick found a new blanket, a sleeper that looked as if it would fit the fussy infant, and helped Sue restore order to her family room.

"How do you know so much about babies born with addictions?" she asked when she was finally sitting back on the couch, fussy baby hiccupping, but asleep in her arms.

"I did some reading."

"Recently?"

"Last night." When thoughts of her were keeping him awake.

"Sonia called today," Sue said after a moment's silence. "She told me about your visitations. Starting Monday."

He nodded. Bit back all the things he wanted to say. About being a father again, about the fact that his mother would be visiting, too. About keeping the woman away from Christy's daughter.

Sue probably knew what he was thinking. But she didn't say anything more, either.

Rick helped with dinner. And baths. Danny and Donnie—he couldn't tell which was which yet, but Sue didn't seem to have that problem—took turns regurgitating their dinner. That was after Sue had finally been able to get the twins to pay enough attention to their bottles to suck from them. They hadn't done much better with the mashed green beans and potatoes. They'd open their tiny mouths, but didn't have much interest in taking the food off the spoon. Or swallowing it once it was dumped on their tongues.

And when all four babies were finally asleep, he followed their foster mother to her kitchen.

"Why don't you go shower and I'll find something to fix you for dinner," he said.

"No way, Kraynick," she retorted, though not with as much vigor as he would normally have expected. "I will not have you waiting on me, spoiling me. And besides, you're the guest and I owe you hugely for tonight and—"

"I'm not waiting on you. I'm concerned about my niece getting proper care when her foster mother is so wiped out she can hardly stand up straight."

Wrapping his arms around her waist, he pulled her close, kissing her softly.

"It's been a long day," Sue said, after returning his kiss with a hunger that had his blood boiling again. "I've had addicted babies before," she said after a couple of seconds of staring at him. "But never in multiples. It'll be fine, though. I'll adjust. I always do."

"I'm not doubting you," he assured her. And he wasn't. "However, you're human. And babies don't understand a long day. I do."

She frowned, but didn't pull out of his arms. "The twins might wake up. As you said, they don't sleep well and—"

"I'll listen for them. And tend to them if they so much as make a peep."

"I don't—"

"Sue," he interrupted, turning her and swatting her bottom. "You could have had your shower and had dinner before you by now, if you'd just go."

"I don't like to be told what to do," she said over her shoulder.

"I figured that out a long time ago."

She stuck out her tongue at him, but without another word headed off down the hall.

Rick spent the next ten minutes scrambling eggs and making toast and trying not to picture his truculent hostess in her shower, naked, with water running down over those luscious breasts.

CHAPTER FOURTEEN

SHE WAS SAFE. She hadn't told him all her secrets. She'd only had sex with him.

Twice.

Great sex.

Fabulous sex.

Sex like she hadn't known sex could be.

But she still had her heart. Control.

And that was the only reason Sue invited Rick back into her bed on Saturday night.

And Sunday night, too. Both times having him arrive after the babies were in bed, and leave before morning.

Rick Kraynick did things to her body she loved. She did not love him. There were no words of commitment between them. No expectation of tomorrow.

She loved his body naked. And probably told him so a few dozen times.

She cared about him. She thought about him all the time. She hadn't even considered calling anyone else for help on Friday when Danny and Donnie were more than she could handle along with Carrie and Michael.

But she did not love him.

A counselor came for Michael Monday morning. And the twins were being flown to the East Coast, to their paternal grandparents, who'd just found out about the babies. She was losing three in one day.

Standing in her living room, with Carrie clutched to her chest, Sue didn't know what to do with herself. She'd never cried over one of her babies before. Never. Not even the first time she had to give one up.

She knew the ropes. Was seasoned.

"Oh, God, what's the matter with me?" she asked aloud.

Seven-month-old Carrie pulled back from her shoulder. Put her hands on Sue's cheeks like she'd done many times before, and frowned.

Because she didn't understand the unfamiliar wetness? Or because she did?

"Oh, baby, I don't know what's the matter with me," she said, choking back another sob.

"Your uncle's coming to see you tonight. You, not me. You're going to officially meet him. He'll get to hold you."

And they hadn't talked about it. At all. Was he nervous about holding Carrie? Afraid she'd remind him of Hannah?

Was he eager to hold her, hoping she'd ease the grief of missing his own daughter?

"I can't hurt another man."

That was her problem. She was afraid of hurting Rick. They were so good together—and together so much, all of a sudden.

But nothing had really changed. She still wasn't going to help him in his custody battle against his mother.

And Sue still wasn't ever going to commit to a permanent relationship.

She didn't know if he'd be sleeping with her that night. Just thinking about him turned her on.

She was feeling tense because she needed him to leave her alone. But she didn't want him to.

Feeling tense because he was making her think about things she'd promised herself never to think about again. To remember things best not remembered. To hurt where she'd stopped hurting a long time ago.

"I'm a mess," she told the adorable little girl in her arms. "You wanna be a mess, too?"

Carrie stared at her.

"Come on. Let's go make some cereal with mashed bananas, and I'll let you try to get some food in your mouth all by yourself."

CHAPTER FIFTEEN

JUST WHEN SUE HAD HERSELF convinced she was ready to face Carrie's uncle, to facilitate his visitation, Joe called.

"My dad said he'd heard from your cousin, Belle," he stated without preamble.

"She's your cousin, too."

His pause was significant. Sue just wasn't sure what it signified. Rejection or difficulty with acceptance?

"She wants us all to get together for dinner."

"I know."

"I don't think it's a good idea."

Sue wasn't surprised. "Why not?"

"It's just too…messy."

She'd give him that.

"I've got enough to deal with with my ex and her fiancé, and seeing Kaitlin, and now my dad in town…."

"I understand." Sort of.

"I was hoping you'd talk to your cousin. Get her to quit calling my dad."

"She's your cousin, too," Sue repeated. And then relented. "So your dad doesn't want anything to do with us, either?"

"I never said I didn't want anything to do with you."

"You didn't have to say it."

"Look, Sue, I—"

"No, I'm sorry I pushed, Joe. I'm just surprised at your dad. I'd have thought, with his coming back to make amends and all, finding out he has more family than he expected would be a good thing. My mom's his sister. His full sister. She really wants to get to know him."

"He wants to know her, too," Joe said with obvious reluctance. "He just won't go to any meetings without me."

Aha. She got it.

"Put the shoe on the other foot, Sue," he said. "If your mother was in town, trying to get all buddy-buddy with you, you'd balk. And she's a great mother!"

He was right. Of course.

"I guess we have some family resemblance," he continued.

"Oh?" She thought she heard a car. Rick? If so, he was half an hour early. His niece was still in her crib, asleep.

And Sue hadn't yet changed out of her banana-smeared T-shirt.

"We're emotionally distant. Kind of like the old man, fathering two children with another woman and then leaving her to struggle alone and to live with the secret of her children's parentage."

"I'm a bit angry with him myself," Sue said. "How could he have raised my mother and never once held her close and told her he was her real father?"

"Because, as I said, he was emotionally detached. Just like you are. And I am."

"He loved us all. From afar," Sue said slowly. And that's what she did. What she'd always done.

Except once. And that time, that mistake, would go with her to her grave.

RICK HAD NO IDEA what to expect out of Monday's visit. He'd seen Sue three nights over the weekend, held her, made love to her, and though she'd been passionate and generous in his arms, she'd also been distant.

They'd talked, but not about anything that really mattered. Not about his mother. Or Carrie. Or the future.

He remembered the previous night, just before he'd gotten up to leave. "I could spend the rest of my life right here," he'd said.

"Don't get too attached, Kraynick." The warning had been couched with teasing, but he'd caught it loud and clear.

"No worries," he'd assured her. But it was already too late.

And on the drive home, he'd made himself face the truth. In some ways, Sue Bookman was Sheila all over again. A woman who needed her space. Who ran from close relationships. Like Sheila, she recognized her needs. Knew herself. But unlike Sheila, she'd been honest with him from the very start.

And maybe Sheila had thought he understood. Maybe in his overeagerness he'd missed her messages. Regardless, he'd been telling himself all day that he was just going to have to stay out of Sue's bed. But a body come back to life didn't care much about the future. It was just glad to be alive again.

As he drove back out to Sue's Monday after work he had to wonder. What was it about him that attracted women who had to get away? First his mother. Then Sheila.

And now Sue.

HE WASN'T GOING TO MAKE a big deal of this. Rick's hands were shaking anyway when he knocked on Sue's door at five minutes before four. He'd seen Carrie a few times already.

He'd *seen* her.

But he hadn't held her. Hadn't so much as fed her a bottle or raised a spoon to her mouth.

Sue was dressed to go out, in pants, a matching black blouse and slip-on shoes, when she answered the door. Her hair was pulled back as usual.

He started to tell her she looked beautiful, but stopped himself. This visit was official. It was about Carrie now.

About Carrie's future.

"Come on in." Sue's smile could have been delivered to a stranger on the street.

"Thanks."

He'd been in the house several times. So why did he suddenly feel so awkward?

"She's in here. In her swing."

Rick felt as though he were entering the room for the first time. He recognized the furniture, the bassinet and toy basket. And it all felt completely new. His gaze went instantly to the baby girl looking around her with curiosity as she gently rocked back and forth in the swing.

His baby sister's baby.

"I'd like to hold her," he said. And then he looked around him. "Where's Michael? And the twins?"

"Gone."

"Gone?" Not again. "As in, we'll never see them again?"

"That's right."

She didn't even blink. Her lack of emotion was chilling.

Until he saw the way her hand was picking at the side of her pants. And Rick wondered, not for the first time, if it wasn't so much that Sue was distant, as that she was lost. So far lost, she couldn't find her way.

Had anyone ever tried to help her?

Sue stopped the swing. Lifting Carrie out, she gently handed the infant to him.

"Hey, sweetie," he said softly as he took the little girl into his arms, smiling easily, when he'd been afraid he'd never get through the moment. "I'm your uncle Rick…" She settled into the crook of his arm as though she'd been born there. Gazed up at him. And smiled back.

RICK FED CARRIE. Sue kept herself busy in the kitchen. Mashing the chicken and ham and peas and broccoli she'd bought at the grocery that afternoon before Joe's call. She put some in the reusable jars she kept in the refrigerator, and the rest in containers for the freezer.

She did the dishes.

And kept an eye on everything that was happening over at the table.

"You're a good girl, Carrie baby." Rick's soft tone brought tears to her eyes. "One more bite for Daddy?"

He wasn't the baby's father yet. He might not ever be. Sue was driving herself crazy with thoughts about him and Carrie. And with trying not to do so.

He wanted the baby. And tonight showed that he could be incredibly gentle and kind with her. But Sue had known he would be. What worried her was that in all of his talk about getting Carrie, he'd never once mentioned that he wanted her for himself, or talked about the joys of being a father. He'd talked about getting Carrie so that he could keep her from his mother, who really did want her and might be a wonderful mom this time around.

Sue also feared that Rick hadn't had time enough to recover from Hannah's death. To deal with that grief. She was afraid he was using Carrie to block it.

"All done!" She listened to him half sing the words. And heard the babbled reply. Carrie was giving her rendition of a giggle. Flirting.

"We're done." Rick appeared in the kitchen archway a couple of seconds later, with Carrie on his hip and her empty bowl in his hand.

Sue met his gaze, connecting to him even while telling herself she wouldn't. "She likes you."

"I hope so. She's amazing."

Sue finished cleaning up, checked the clock and reached for her charge. "Bath time," she said.

Rick didn't let go.

"Your visitation was from four to five. It's five after." She was being a bitch. She wasn't proud of that fact. But she couldn't give him special favors. Visitations times were strictly adhered to.

Rick turned over the infant. "May I at least stay to kiss her good-night?"

She tried to tell him no. But those green eyes held depths she understood. And couldn't deny. "Yes." And if Nancy Kraynick asked to stay past visiting hour, she'd grant her request, too.

Sue was an emotional mess when Rick followed her out to the living room after she'd put Carrie down for the night.

How had she ever thought they could separate "them" from "him and Carrie"? As though he was two different people.

Or she was.

"Okay, that's done," he said, standing in the middle of the room. "Visitation's over. Can I just be Rick again?"

If only it were that easy.

Or in any way possible.

"I don't know how to do that," Sue told him. "I mean, what are we doing here? Being playmates? For how long? When does it end? How do we know when it's time?"

"I'm okay with playmates, if that works for you."

Of course it didn't work for her. Was the man an idiot?

If he was, he was no more idiotic than she'd been. She stood with her back to him, trying to decide what to do next. Disinfect the changing table, put clean sheets on the bassinet or rearrange the furniture. "I'm not a toy."

"Sue." He took her hand, pulled her around to face him. "I was merely repeating your words back at you."

She studied him. And nodded.

"I don't mind being your playmate, but I am also your friend and whatever else you'll let me be."

"See," she said, making herself face him down before she started to cry again, "that's the problem with you. You don't know how to keep your distance."

"I thought that was your job."

Damn him. Did he have to be so...so...

Right?

"Look, Rick, I'm tired. The twins took more out of me than I realized. And I've got accounting work to do. It's probably best if you go. For tonight."

She'd almost made it sound final. Almost.

But then, he'd be back on Wednesday, regardless of what happened between the two of them. He was visiting Carrie. And she was an employee of the agency that had custody of the child.

"I..." He ran the back of his fingers down her face, stopping short of her collarbone.

Sue turned her head, holding his hand captive between her cheek and shoulder.

"What's going on, sweetie?" he asked. "What happened between last night and tonight?"

Babies leaving. Reminding her that everything was temporary. Because she needed it that way. Joe's call. Rick needing Carrie. Her needing him.

"Nothing. I'm just confused about what we're doing here. That's all." She released his hand, but he didn't move it.

"I'm a little confused myself." He rubbed his thumb along her lips. "I get the feeling that we're not in control as much as we think we are."

"Me, too. And I can't have that."

"So let's take control. You wanted to know when and how it ends? Let's decide."

Had he found a way out for them? A solution? "How do you decide something like that? We'll know each other until Christmas and then go our separate ways? Or until one of us gets bored? Or do we just say we'll be friends until Carrie's future is decided?"

None of the options seemed credible. Or acceptable.

"Why don't we just let go of the outcome. We understand each other's boundaries. Let's abide by them."

She had to get rid of him before she let him in any further. He was already dangerously close to trespassing on sacred ground.

"Your mother's coming tomorrow," Sue stated.

"I know. At seven."

"You do?"

"Yes."

"Since when?"

"Friday."

"You knew all weekend."

"Yes."

"And you didn't say anything?"

"Did you?"

Well, no, she hadn't. Because it hadn't been her place. She was entrusted by the state to keep information regarding her charges confidential.

He wasn't under any such stipulations.

"Who told you?" Had he talked to his mother and not told her?

"Sonia."

Sue should have figured it out. Would have if she wasn't so damned upside down on this one. She was losing control. Losing clarity.

She had to take charge here.

"It's my job to help your mom acclimate. To do anything I can to facilitate her ability to be a good mother to Carrie."

"You're so bound and determined to throw my mother in my face. I'm beginning to wonder if you aren't playing favorites, after all. I'm just not the favorite."

Shocked that he'd even think such a thing, Sue stared. She wanted to argue. To deny his accusation. And was even more shocked when she couldn't. Was he right? Was she overcompensating?

"My report to the committee will be fair," she assured him. "I paid close attention to your visit tonight."

"Uh-huh." He slid his hands in the pockets of his pants. "And how'd I do?"

"Great. You're a natural at handling a baby."

"And?"

"Your situation reminds me of my mother's," she

started. "She grew up without that sense of being a full-fledged member of a family. She was always on the outside looking in. She got to live with them, call herself one of them, but it was never quite the real deal. Like you, in all those foster homes. You could pretend you were a member of the family, but you always knew you weren't."

"What's your point?"

"Look what that did to my mother. The same thing it sounds like it did to you. As soon as you were out on your own, you found a relationship and wanted to get married, to raise a family, to have a family of your own."

His eyes narrowed. "Yeah."

"Not like most people want families. You want an all-consuming relationship. Just like my mother. Except that she was a little luckier when she met my dad then you were with Sheila. Because my dad wanted the same thing she did."

"Again, what's your point?"

"You want Carrie to be your all-consuming family."

"I believe family is everything, yes."

"I don't want you to have her because of the risk that she'd grow up like I did. You'd smother her. Suffocate her. Especially after having lost Hannah."

He looked as though she'd slapped him. "That's unfair."

"Maybe," she conceded. "But look how much you've been here. We've only known each other a few weeks and you're practically living with us."

He pulled back, his entire countenance stiffening.

"I thought you wanted me here." His eyes held no warmth at all.

She had. She did. And that was a big part of the problem. Not his, though. Hers.

"What I want is beside the point. I just think you have too many issues to be good for Carrie. You've been hurt so much. You can't see your mother clearly. Can't give her the benefit of the doubt, and I understand why. But that doesn't make it good for Carrie. And then there's Hannah. You have so many scars...."

"And my mother doesn't?"

"I don't know. I haven't met her yet."

"Well, give me a call after you do," he said, heading for the door. "Or better yet, don't. Maybe you're right. Maybe we need time apart to figure out what we're doing here. I'll see you Wednesday at four."

Before she could come up with a reply, he was gone.

CHAPTER SIXTEEN

"WHAT'S UP, MAN?" MARK huffed as he went for the rebound.

"Why does anything have to be up?" Rick was first to the ball. Took it back.

"A Tuesday afternoon game is a sure sign that something's wrong." Mark stayed right on him, his hands filling the space around him.

"I needed the exercise."

"Bullshit."

That reminded him of Sue. Of her response when he'd said it one time. But then, for the past two days, everything reminded him of Sue.

And Carrie.

"How about dinner?" he asked when he'd made the basket. "Think Darla would agree to meet us someplace?"

"Probably." Mark grabbed the ball, made a basket, rebounded and brought the ball down to hold it. "She's waiting for my call," he admitted. "Waiting to hear what's going on."

"Have her meet us at Tally's," Rick said, naming a bar and grill not far from their homes.

While Mark called his wife, Rick went in to shower.

"Ms. Kraynick, please, come in." Sue smiled as she opened her door to the woman, who was much younger looking than she'd expected.

"Thank you." Nancy Kraynick could have been a seventies sit-com remake in her conservative pants and blouse, her flat shoes, tasteful makeup and understated, short dark hairstyle.

Her handshake was firm and she looked Sue straight in the eye. "You've already met my son," she said. "Sonia told me he was here yesterday."

"Yes." And with those green eyes, she was the spitting image of him.

"He's not all that fond of me."

"I wouldn't say that."

"It's all right, Ms. Bookman. Whether Ricky realizes it or not, I know my son."

Sue liked the woman. She couldn't help it; she just did. "Please call me Sue."

She moved toward the family room, where Carrie waited in her swing.

"I want to tell you," Nancy said, "up front, that anything my son told you about me is right. Ricky doesn't lie."

"Okay."

"But he hasn't seen me in years. He doesn't believe I've changed, but I have, Ms. Bookman. I am not the woman who let him down. I need a chance to prove that to him."

Other than being a little on the thin side, the woman didn't look anything like an addict. Her complexion was rosy and healthy looking. Her eyes were clear.

"Well, maybe you'll get your chance," Sue told her. She hoped so. But didn't count on it. "Now, would you like to see your granddaughter?"

"Oh, yes. You have no idea how badly."

Nancy's grasp was confident when Sue handed the baby to her. And when Carrie looked up and smiled, the older woman's eyes filled with tears. "Hello again, my precious princess," she said. "Grandma's back and she's going to be here for good this time. She's got a room already prepared for you. A crib and a changing table, drawers full of clothes, a basket of toys…."

Sue supervised the visit—as she had done with Rick the night before—and knew that her lover's chances of being granted his adoption were dwindling. Nancy Kraynick was wonderful.

And prepared.

As far as Sue knew, Rick hadn't even thought about a box of disposable diapers, let alone a fully stocked nursery.

RICK WAITED UNTIL Darla and Mark had beers in front of them. "I got the stay and I'm moving forward with the adoption proceedings. I had my physical today." He hadn't even had a sip of his iced tea. Or looked at the menu to decide what he wanted for dinner.

Dinner didn't much matter. Any food would do.

Mark frowned.

"Oh, Rick, are you sure?" Darla asked.

"Yeah, I'm sure. I had my first visit with her yesterday." His mother was having hers at that exact moment.

Was Sue dressed in her "greeting" clothes? Filling his mother in on all of Carrie's likes and dislikes? Her progress since his mother had last seen the baby, hours after her birth? Was she going to let his mom give Carrie her bath? And kiss her good-night?

Was she telling Nancy that she didn't think Rick was the best choice for Carrie? Telling her that she'd help her, where she'd told Rick she couldn't?

"How'd it go?" Darla asked, exchanging a glance with her husband as though Rick wasn't sitting right there, able to note their obvious concern.

"Good. Great. The second I picked her up, she looked at me and smiled." He remembered how wonderful that had felt. "I fed her and that was about it. My time was up. But I go back tomorrow."

And he wasn't going to let Sue Bookman get to him when he did. This was about Carrie now.

"So what happens next?" Mark asked.

"The agency conducts a thorough investigation. Medical records, criminal records, employment records. They inspect my home, my finances, my lifestyle." And his mother's. But he didn't tell his friends that part. Carrie was not going to his mother. "Once that's done, they'll issue an order to place her in my home. They continue to monitor us for up to six months and then the court grants the adoption." It was a simplified version of the process, but accurate.

"I can't believe you're really doing this," Mark said.

"What happens if you change your mind?" Darla asked.

"Would you two please quit looking at me like I'm an alien? I'm not going to change my mind. I'm not crazy. I know, clearly and calmly, that this is the right thing for me to do."

"You haven't even cleaned out Hannah's room."

"Yes, I have."

"You did?" his friends asked simultaneously.

"Last night. I had to make room for the new nursery equipment I had delivered this afternoon. I wanted her in the room across from me, so I can hear her if she wakes in the night."

The room across from him. Hannah's room. He'd had a long talk with his daughter about that during the early hours of that morning.

"What did you do with her stuff?"

"Put it in the spare bedroom." Exactly as it had been in Hannah's room. Or as much the same as it had been physically possible to make it. "Carrie might want some or all of it."

The point was valid.

"Look, I've still got a long way to go in dealing with Hannah's death. But this is the right thing to do. I'm ready to move on. To start over. I don't think it's any mistake that Carrie came into my life when she did. She needs a parent. And I was a great dad. More than that, I loved being a parent."

Mark and Darla studied him. He withstood the scrutiny with ease.

Mark was the first to relent. "We're here for you if you need anything, you know that, right?"

"Of course. That works both ways."

Mark picked up his menu. "So, what sounds good for dinner?"

When their plates were empty and they'd covered every topic any of them could think of beside babies, Hannah and Rick's state of mind, Mark reached for the bill.

"I've got this one," Rick said.

And as they were walking out the door, Darla leaned over and asked, "Do you need a sitter? I'd be thrilled to have a baby in the house again."

Though they'd been trying for years, Mark and Darla had yet to conceive a child of their own.

"I'd appreciate the help," he told his friend. "I was going to get around to asking. I just wanted to give you time to realize I wasn't completely insane, first."

"Oh, Rick, we haven't ever thought that. You're the most together guy I've ever met," she said. "You're hurting, that's all. And it's our job to have your back while you do."

It was after eight o'clock. His mother's time was up. Rick drove home with mixed emotions. He missed Sue. But he was far richer than he'd dared to remember. He might not have a family living in his home yet, but he had a great job and true friends.

All in all, Rick was a very lucky man.

SUE FINISHED THE WORK due to Joe's office in the morning. Put in a call to arrange courier pickup at eight. She checked on Carrie for the third time. Finished the laundry. There were fresh sheets on the three vacant cribs.

She called her parents, who were home. And Belle, who wasn't. She read old birthday cards from Grandma Sarah. And tried to look at pictures of her, but couldn't.

She carried her phone into the kitchen to pour a glass of tea, with Rick's number in her head. She was not going to call him. He'd be there in less than twenty-four hours. As a potential adoptive parent.

Which was as it had to be.

As she wanted it to be.

Too restless to settle in front of the TV, too wired to go to bed, unable to concentrate on the book she'd started six months ago, she ended up in her bathroom, filling the tub with the relaxation crystals Belle had bought her last Christmas, and got undressed.

She thought about Rick, and the last time she'd had a long soak in the tub. Her phone was on the counter, but she was not going to call him.

But if he called—because he probably needed to know how his mother's visit had transpired that night—she'd answer. She'd talk to him.

Be nice to him.

Maybe even apologize for being too outspoken the day before.

He might be willing to be friends with her even though she couldn't help him with Carrie. He'd been willing before.

The thought comforted her. They'd had something special. He'd call.

He didn't call.

Sue went to bed with a depression that seared her to the bone.

RICK HEARD AN unfamiliar cry when he approached Sue's place Wednesday afternoon. Someone was hurt. Someone little.

He knocked and then tried the door. It was locked, but Sue was there, crying baby at her shoulder, unlocking it.

"Sorry," she said, meeting his gaze almost shyly for a brief second. "He's not feeling well."

"What's wrong with him?"

Sue had turned while he was asking the question, and he caught a glimpse of the baby's face. "What *happened* to him?"

The vision of his daughter's accident spun through his mind. But this child was alive. The baby was crying.

"His father."

"His father what?" *Died in the crash?*

"Jake's father didn't like it when he told his son to be quiet and Jake didn't do it." Sue shuddered. Inhaled. "He decided to teach him discipline."

The entire left side of the baby's face was discolored. Swollen. "Is he going to be okay?"

"Yeah, they say he got lucky." Sue kissed the unharmed side of the baby's face, murmuring in his ear, and then said, "He's got a couple of broken ribs. And lots of bruises, but no internal injuries. And no brain damage. Thank God."

She seemed to be taking it all so calmly. But then she wasn't looking him in the eye, so it was hard to tell what was really going on with her.

Rick was trying not to puke.

"How old is he?"

"Three months."

"Three months old and his own father did this to him?"

"Yeah. Crazy world we live in, isn't it?"

"People really are capable of anything, aren't they?"

"Some people are."

Rick didn't get it. He didn't want to get it. He wanted to grab Carrie and take her home. To protect her from every ugly thing that existed in the world. To keep her safe and secluded and alive.

Which was exactly what Sue had accused him of wanting to do. Suffocating her.

She let him bathe Carrie after dinner, standing over him with Jake in her arms. And she followed him into the nursery to watch as he kissed the girl and laid her gently on her back. "Sweet dreams and God's care, little one," he whispered. Just as he'd done every single night of Hannah's life. And as he'd do every single night he put any children, present or future, to bed. Some things were just that important.

As he turned, Sue met his gaze for the first time that night. Her eyes were bright with tears.

"I…"

"Shhh." He indicated the crib. "It's okay."

And it was. Whatever *it* was. He walked behind her into the hall.

"I guess I'll be going," he said, but he didn't move. "Unless...do you need some help bathing him?"

Maybe, with his help, she could wash the baby without applying pressure to his injury.

"I..." She looked at him and then away. "Thanks," she said, heading toward the bathroom again, and the infant bath secured inside the tub. As soon as he was inside, she turned back to Rick.

"Prepare yourself."

He'd been looking at the little guy's face all night. He was prepared. Or thought he was. Until she unsnapped the sleeper covering Jake's discolored and misshapen body. Then he made a dash for the toilet and threw up.

CHAPTER SEVENTEEN

SUE LAY BACK in the chair in her family room, Jake lying on her chest, sound asleep. She'd changed into a soft cotton pajama top and flannel pants an hour before, while Rick made them a salad and toast for dinner. She'd tried to resist, but Carrie was in bed. She wasn't playing favorites. And tonight she needed a friend.

She needed Rick.

With one hand resting gently at Jake's back, she reassured the unconscious child that he was safe. Her heartbeat beneath his little body would hopefully do the same.

"What happened to his mother?" Rick asked, tie gone and the top two buttons of his dress shirt undone as he lounged in a corner of the couch.

Like he was going to stay awhile. Sue wasn't going to tell him to leave.

"She's in rehab."

His expression didn't outwardly change, but Sue felt the tension emanating from him. "Let me guess," he said calmly, "she won't sign papers to give him up."

"She's trying to get herself clean."

"Umm-hmm." He had the air of one who'd seen it all too many times before. And he had. But...

"Everyone deserves a chance, Rick," she said, more desperate after meeting Nancy Kraynick to open him to the possibility. If he couldn't get this point, every one of them could lose. Carrie, Nancy, him. Sue. "I've seen and heard of many cases where the birth of a child is the miracle a misguided person needed. Not everyone who does drugs is addicted for life. Not everyone falls back."

"Got any statistics on that?"

Her heart sank. "No." But she had a feeling he did.

"Last year's stats say that only 58.2 to 69.1 percent of clean addicts stay sober."

He wasn't simply reacting emotionally and irrationally to his mother's petition for adoption, based on his own experience. He'd done his homework.

Rick Kraynick was a fair man.

He just wasn't always right.

"That's over half, Rick. Which means a good many second chances end happily."

"Tell that to Jake," Rick said softly, pinning her with a half-lidded stare. "Tell him that you're willing to take a 41.9 percent chance that he'll be beat up again."

"People aren't statistics, Rick," Sue said. "Society tries to make us numbers, to give us numbers, call us by numbers, judge us by numbers, but we'll never be numbers. Every single one of us is an individual with a unique set of circumstances. And not one of us is the same today as we were ten years ago." She was afraid she sounded like a psychology textbook. But he had to get this. He just had to. "Those circumstances shape who we are. They change people. And no one's perfect. Everyone screws up. We've got to be able to give second chances. To get them. Or we're all doomed."

"We aren't talking about everyday mistakes, Sue. And you're kidding yourself if you think Carrie isn't a case number. Jake is, too. And all the other children that pass through here."

"Their paperwork is assigned a case number for filing purposes. The children are not numbers. Think about what you're saying…." She had to keep her voice down, her heart steady, for the sake of her precious little guest. "If we just went by numbers, we lose everything human about us. You're negating the most important factor here, Rick."

And not just concerning Carrie, though it did concern her. Greatly.

"What's that?"

"Heart." She met his gaze, silently begging him.

So far, Nancy Kraynick—and they both knew that was who they were talking about—had impressed her. Sue had a feeling the grandmother, not yet fifty years old, was never going to forgive herself for the mistakes she'd made in her life.

"Your mother learned hard lessons," she dared to venture. "And sometimes it's the hardest lessons that serve us the best."

"Forgive me if I'm not much interested in my mother's lessons learned," Rick said, sitting forward. "Not when my little sister's no longer on this earth because of her."

"So the parents are to blame for every kid that commits suicide?"

"You think if Christy had a loving, attentive, *sober* mother at home she'd have been buying drugs off the streets and been pregnant at age fifteen?"

"It happens."

He stood. "This is getting us nowhere."

He was right. It wasn't. But it felt right having him there. Like he was part of the room. Of the household.

Of her life?

"Just for the record," he said, slipping back into the shoes he'd kicked off when he sat down, "I think what Jo Fraser did, giving your mother up for adoption, was one of the most incredible, selfless and loving acts I've ever heard of. She must have known the life she had to give your mother would have been hard. And it seems to me that she loved her enough to sacrifice herself, her own happiness and needs, to give her daughter the best chance at life."

"My mother grew up feeling as though she never really belonged. If Jo had kept her, she'd have not only belonged, she'd have probably had a brother who loved her, who was her friend, rather than one who always resented her."

"Maybe. Or she might have been a teenager buying drugs on the streets."

"Jo did great by Adam. And by Daniel and Joe, too."

"But none of them were considered illegitimate. I'm guessing from what you've said that their family was thought of with compassion. Respected. They had assistance and support from good families, opportunities at school. Add Jenny to that mix and not only does she become the bastard child, but Jo's reputation would have been tarnished, the opportunities would have been fewer and the boys would have suffered, too. Their lives might have been completely different."

"Maybe." Sue wasn't going to stand. Wasn't going to see him out. She didn't want him to go.

"And even if your uncle wasn't the best of brothers, wasn't good to your mother, that happens in families everywhere," he told her. "I see it often enough in the schools. You'll have three kids in a family who are great. They excel in academics and sports, have a lot of nice friends and obviously love each other. And then there will be one who keeps the parents up at night."

Sue didn't want him to be right.

Because she was right, too.

Which meant they were forever going to be on opposite sides of the fence.

So where did that leave them?

And where did it leave Carrie?

RICK WAS ALMOST AT the front door when he thought he heard a noise at the back of the house, down the hall by the vacant nursery where Danny and Donnie had slept.

He stopped. Listened. Told himself he was imagining things. And to get out.

He heard it again. Not a bang. Not quite a tapping. More like a grinding.

Moving quietly so he could listen, he turned back to

the family room, to see if Sue had heard anything. With her head facing down the hall, she was slowly rising from her chair, both arms wrapped around the baby still asleep against her.

She glanced his way when he got close. And the fear he read in her eyes had adrenaline speeding through him.

She'd heard something, too. And whatever caused it was obviously not a familiar house sound that Sue could explain away.

"You stay here with him," he barely whispered, leaning right up to her ear. "And call 911."

Sue nodded, shielding the baby and sending Rick a silent plea. One he instantly understood. Jake was safe. But Carrie was in the back of the house.

Grabbing a candlestick off the mantel, the only thing close by that offered any protection in the baby-proofed room, Rick moved stealthily down the hall, keeping as much to the wall as he could. He recalled an old board game he'd played as a kid. *Colonel Mustard with the candlestick in the ballroom...* But he'd rather overreact and have everyone safe than be taken unawares.

He heard the sound again, on the right side of the hall. And it was definitely grinding. Like someone, or something, was gnawing at wood. Or prying wood.

A squirrel maybe. Or a coyote?

Sue's bedroom door, on the left side of the hall, was open. She'd left a light on. Her curtains were drawn, but what he could see of the room appeared undisturbed.

"Yes, that's right..." Sue's voice was faint in the distance, reciting her address.

The twins' nursery was next. It, too, as much as he could tell from a brief glance into a darkened room from the dimly lit hallway, appeared empty.

His goal was Carrie. Once he knew the little girl was safe, he'd be more thorough in his exploration of the rest of the house.

His niece was in her crib, exactly as he'd left her. Lying on her side, sound asleep. The mobile above the crib had stopped.

He heard the sound again. Behind him. Between him and the family room. This time more clearly. It was rhythmic, and accompanied by a slight squeak.

Someone *was* prying something.

Candlestick in hand, Rick slid his free arm underneath the sleeping baby, scooping her up into the protective cover of his arm and chest, like a football.

With the child safe against him, Rick's concern diminished. If someone was breaking in, surely he'd be more swift about it, and a little quieter?

Taking Carrie to Sue, who now had Jake strapped to her chest in a baby carrier, he settled the little girl into her foster mother's arms. "I didn't see anything," he murmured quietly. "But the sound is definitely coming from back there. I'm going to go take a second look."

She nodded, her face still lined with concern. "The police are on their way. Just in case."

Rick stopped at Sue's door. Made a quick check of the bathroom adjoining her room, and didn't see anything that could explain the noise. He headed for the unused nursery. He hadn't heard the sound since he'd returned from the family room.

It was the last thought Rick had before something blunt and hard came down against his left collarbone, followed by excruciating pain.

Instinctively, he swung his movable arm, his right arm. The hand with the candlestick. And heard a grunt as he felt a connection.

Still reacting without thinking, Rick threw himself toward the noise, toward a shadow just inside the door of the empty nursery. He landed on top of a wiry, obviously male body that was shorter than his, but just as strong.

"Give it up, you son of a bitch," he said, hardly aware of the pain searing his left shoulder as he realized that Sue had been in very real danger. Sue and her babies.

"Not…without…my…*sssson,*" the man hissed, his breath laced with the smell of liquor. "He's mine. I want him."

With a shove against Rick's left shoulder, the man rolled the two of them, until he was on top. But using the momentum the other man had started, Rick managed to get the guy back underneath him.

Dropping the candlestick to get ahold of one of the man's arms, he brought his knee up for a quick slice to the groin and, bracing against the pain in his shoulder, grabbed for the intruder's other hand.

That hand held a gun.

"Hold it right there."

The light flashed on and Rick briefly registered Sue

standing in the doorway, alone, with her own gun pointed straight at the head of the man beneath him. Keeping hold of the man's wrists, Rick shifted so that he was out of range of her shot. And held on.

"Drop the gun."

The man fought, kicking and pushing against Rick, who fought right back. He had babies at stake. And a woman he cared about a great deal. This son of a bitch was not getting away from him.

"I'd do as she says," he told the man, able to hold him so that the gun pointed to a back wall. The weapon went off.

Rick banged the man's wrist against the floor. And the gun went off again.

He saw the black shoes on the floor beside him before he realized that they had guests. Welcome guests.

Not sure how he ended up standing next to Sue while two uniformed officers handcuffed the man he'd been wrestling with, Rick was only thankful that no one had been hurt.

"Oh, my God, Rick, your arm. What happened?"

"Nothing, it's fine." He could hardly feel it.

"Not the way it's hanging, it isn't. Officer, can you call an ambulance?"

"There's already one here."

CHAPTER EIGHTEEN

SUE DIDN'T EXPECT TO SEE Rick again that night. She'd listened carefully to the officer's instructions to make sure to lock her door behind them, but, while still shaken by what had happened, she wasn't afraid of any further danger. Jake's father, who'd found a way to post a $50,000 bond earlier that day and had broken into Social Services to get his son's record, was now locked up again. Without bail.

She hoped for a good long time.

No longer scared, she'd still rolled the babies' bassinets into her room. And figured she'd probably be awake the rest of the night. There was something daunting about giving up consciousness when it was still dark outside and you'd just had an intruder.

Maybe that was why she was lying under the covers, still dressed in the jeans she'd put on after the officers left, with her cell phone in her hand.

She answered on the first ring, because it was Rick calling.

"I'm coming up the street. Will you let me in?"

"Of course. I...how'd you get here?" His SUV was still in her drive.

"A cab."

He'd phoned from the hospital. Told her he had a broken collarbone and that, other than wrap his arm in a sling, there was little they could do about it. He'd said he was fine. But nothing about coming over. She'd thought he was staying there for the rest of the night.

"I'll meet you at the door."

HE DIDN'T LOOK NEARLY AS good as he said he felt. His face ashen, his hair disheveled and his eyes reflecting the pain he wasn't admitting to feeling, Rick stood stiffly in his wrinkled work shirt and pants. "I had to come get my car, and couldn't go home without making sure you and the kids were all right."

Sue crossed her arms. "You aren't going home, and don't bother wasting your energy on argument," she said. "If you think I'm going to have you driving like this, you're nuts."

Rick swayed. "They put something for pain in my IV," he admitted. "I was thinking about sleeping it off in my car."

Because he didn't think he could ask her for help? Sue had to clasp both hands behind her back to keep from touching him, reassuring herself that he was all right. That she was.

"Do you need anything to drink?"

"No." He handed her some papers. Instructions for him. Instructions she was going to read and follow just as soon as she had him out of his torn clothes and lying down, so she didn't have to worry about him falling down. "I'm…are the babies okay? Can I see them?"

"They're fine." She checked the front door one more time and then, with the papers in one hand, slid the other around his back and led him down the hall to her room.

She needed him in her bed tonight, close enough to touch, close enough to hear if he wanted anything.

But even with Rick sound asleep next to her, an ice pack on his wound, and the babies' breathing clearly audible on either side of the bed, Sue lay wide-eyed, staring at the ceiling.

TWO WEEKS OF WEARING a sling was too much for Rick. He had no idea how he was going to stand two months of the torture. He'd much prefer to not wear the sling and suffer any consequential pain.

Except that he didn't want the bone to heal crookedly.

So as he let the agency people into his home, to score through all of his private details, as he submitted to interviews, went to work, he wore the damn sling.

He wore it on his visitation nights, when he held and fed Carrie.

The only exception he made, the only time he didn't have the cotton strapped across his chest, other than when he showered, were the few times he made love to Sue. He refused to have anything between his skin and hers.

They already had too much between them.

Friday, April 10, nine days after the break-in, the day his mother was to have had her final interview with the agency and either be rewarded or denied placement, the six-month trial period before the final adoption, passed without event. Because of Rick being in the picture, her appointment had been postponed.

He thought about calling her. But didn't. There was no point in caring about her needs. It always ended with her no longer sober and his heart deader than the last time.

Sonia, Carrie's caseworker, called him the following Wednesday, exactly two weeks after the break-in at Sue's.

Rick closed his office door as he answered the call, and then, instead of returning to his desk, moved over to the fourth-floor window across from it and gazed out at the sunny day and down to the people briskly moving on the sidewalk below.

His heart pounding, he interrupted her spiel about procedures and policies. "Have you made a decision?" he asked, holding the phone with the hand he could raise to ear level. *Please, God, let this one go right. Please. Save a baby. Just one baby.*

"Not yet." He started to breathe again. "But I am calling to warn you, Mr. Kraynick, that we're leaning more toward your mother."

Funny how tension could return in a split second. "How could you be?"

"Because she meets all the requirements. Her scores are all above average…."

Scores. So much for Sue's assertion that they didn't look at numbers. "What scores?"

"When we do our assessments we assign scores to each area of interest and concern. Your mother has only two drawbacks. Her age, which isn't really even a consideration—she's just a little older than the average parent receiving a baby. And her past drug use. But she's shown very clearly that that use is in the past."

Rick had an idea that the caseworker shouldn't really have been giving him this information. So why was she?

Because she really wanted Rick to have Carrie and was looking for a way to help him?

Or because she felt sorry for him?

"Your scores are also fine," she added. "Better than fine, actually. Based on scores only, I'd like to place the baby with you," she continued. And Rick waited for the "but."

"We have an unusual—for us—situation here, Mr. Kraynick. We have two good candidates both related to our charge. So we ask ourselves, looking at the overall picture, who stands to make the most impact on the child?"

Carrie. Her name is Carrie.

"I'm not going to give you all of the strengths and weaknesses we've weighed," Sonia continued, "the pros and cons of each side. I'll just break it down for you this way. You're a single male. Your mother's female. The child is female."

"Single men adopting children is quite common in the state of California." He could quote her the statistics, but had a feeling she already knew them. And that they didn't matter here.

"But not when there is an equally good candidate, a

grandmother who is still almost young enough to be having a child of her own, as an option."

"So what are you telling me? That if I were married, I'd get her?"

"Yes. You're younger. You've had the same job for a longer period of time. Your neighborhood is nicer. You were a stellar parent in the past...."

Frustration, like bile, rose in him. "And all of that isn't enough to counteract the fact that I was born male?"

"Your mother showed a much stronger desire to have the child simply because she wanted her," Sonia said.

You only want her so your mom can't have her. Sue's words.

"And we were also concerned about your lack of in-ability to clean out your daughter's room. To pack her stuff away. That indicates you're still in early stages of grief, and perhaps not as emotionally stable as we'd like...."

He grieved. Hell, yes, he grieved. He'd lost a daughter. Tragically. And far too young. A part of him would be grieving for the rest of his life.

But he wasn't nuts. Or unstable. Or even depressed.

"That wasn't her room. That was the spare bedroom." He heard himself excusing what they'd found. "Her room was the one across from mine. The one with the crib now. Carrie's crib. So I can hear her when she wakes in the night...."

Maybe it was time to call Darla and have her help him sort through Hannah's things.

He resisted the thought. Pushed away the vision.

And then in his mind's eye, he saw Sue there, in Hannah's room, helping him….

"So you see, while we haven't come to any conclusions yet, I feel as though we're getting close and I…well…the question has come up, you're sure there's no significant other in your life? Someone who would be playing a significant role in the child's life? Someone we could interview?"

"There's no one."

Sonia sighed. "I have another question."

"What's that?"

"If you were granted placement, would you allow your mother to visit the child?"

He bit the inside of his mouth, his fist clenched in the sling. He didn't want that woman anywhere near Carrie. Didn't anyone get that? Was he the only one in the city who knew what a danger Nancy Kraynick was to anyone who cared about her? To anyone she cared about?

"Mr. Kraynick?"

His mother was Carrie's grandmother. "Yes, ma'am. I would."

"Then let me ask you something else. Have you tried talking to your mother?"

"About what?"

"It seems clear that both of you have the best interests of your young niece at heart," she said. "You both want what's best for the baby. We thought that, perhaps, if it were possible for the two of you to talk, you could work out a solution between the two of you."

"You mean like shared parenting?"

"Not really," she said. "We'll only be granting placement with one of you. Obviously, it's not the best solution for the baby to live in a split home, since we can avoid it. But maybe you can work out something similar to the state's standard visitation order…."

He was shaking his head before she had half the sentence out. "I don't think so." He tried to temper his tone. "First and foremost, because I wouldn't be able to believe or trust any agreement my mother made. And, unlike you, I'm not willing to take any more chances on her."

"Very well, Mr. Kraynick, I really do understand. And thank you. As I said, no decision has been made at this time. If anything changes for you, please let me know. And in the meantime, we'll continue to monitor visitations. I'll be in touch…."

Rick pushed the end button on his phone and stood there, cell clutched in his fist, until he figured out the only solution.

BECAUSE THE BABIES WERE particularly easy on Wednesday, Sue prepared one of Grandma Sarah's favorite dishes—chicken breasts wrapped with bacon and cooked with a chipped beef, cream cheese and mushroom soup sauce, served over rice—to offer Rick after that evening's visitation.

She wasn't domesticating. But other than a couple of late nights when he'd called and she'd invited him over, she'd seen almost nothing of him other than Carrie's visitations. She missed him.

And she'd heard from Sonia today.

Rick still wasn't budging about his mother.

Which wasn't Sue's problem. On this issue, Carrie's best placement could be her only concern. Not helping Rick. Or worrying about him.

So how did she stand back and watch her lover get hurt?

CHAPTER NINETEEN

SUE SPOONED mushroom and cream cheese sauce over the chicken and rice later that night. She'd caught Rick watching her several times during his hour with Carrie.

And he'd seemed relieved when she'd invited him for dinner.

He hadn't said a word about Sonia. But then, neither of them had mentioned his mother, or Carrie's placement, since the break-in.

"We're going to have to talk about it, you know," she said as she laid a plate in front of him and sat down.

"Talk about what?"

"Everything we've been avoiding. Your mother. Carrie. You and me. Whatever it is that's got us here... together...it's not going to make the rest of the world disappear. And neither is running away. We've got serious issues between us."

Rick took a bite, his left hand limp in his lap. His shoulder must hurt. He'd probably overdone it with Carrie. "This is delicious," he said simply.

"Thank you." She waited.

He cleared his plate without another word. Sue barely made inroads on hers.

And when the dishes were done he took her hand, leading her into the living room. She was glad she hadn't eaten much. Her stomach was in knots.

Rick took off his suit coat, laying it over the back of a chair before he joined her on the couch. "I heard from Sonia today," he said.

Sue wasn't ready. She'd asked for this, and she wasn't ready. She was going to lose him. Tucking her bare feet beneath her, she picked at a string in the seam of her jeans. "I know. I did, too."

Eyes narrowed, he watched her, the six inches between them seeming more like six miles. "So you know no decision has been made yet?" he asked slowly.

"Yes. But they're getting close. You scored well."

"Based on what Sonia said to me, there seems to be only one solution to this mess."

That his mother get custody and he agree to court-sanctioned visitations that would guarantee him the same rights as a divorced father—every other weekend and one night during the week, without being required to pay support.

Sue's heart ached for him.

Suddenly exhausted, she wanted to go to bed. To lose herself in Rick's arms. And then wake up and take care of her charges.

"Sue?"

"Yeah?"

"Did you hear anything I just said?"

"Yeah. You said there's only one solution."

"After that. I asked you to marry me."

She sat still, knowing she'd probably heard him the first time around.

"In the first place, you'd be able to keep Carrie. Forever. She'd really be yours. And if we marry only for Carrie's sake, it wouldn't be the kind of all-in partnership you fear. Although, for obvious reasons, health and example to the kids being the most obvious, I'd require fidelity, but considering our inability to keep our hands off each other for more than a few days, I don't see that as presenting much of a problem…."

Sue tried to concentrate on watching his lips move, instead of on processing the words coming out of them, as tension crawled up from her toes, through her legs, into her belly and continued to rise. And spread.

"We make a perfect team," he was saying, "as evidenced by the way we handled Jake's dad a couple of weeks ago. Not to mention Carrie. And then there was Camden, the shooter, and…"

He wasn't saying all of this. He just wasn't.

"We both love kids," Rick continued. "Think of how much more you'd get done having a second set of hands around here to help out with them. And to hold you on the nights after they leave…." He licked his lips. They were full. And masculine at the same time. And the way they felt when he opened them against hers…

"Sue?"

"Yeah?"

"Say something."

He was still just six inches away. Turned toward her.

She could remove his loosened tie, unbutton his shirt from where she sat. Lay her head against his chest.

"I thought you understood," she said. "I can't help you make sure your mother doesn't get Carrie."

That's all this was.

"I won't be taking her from my mother," he said. "I told you, I've already agreed that if I do get placement, my mother will be allowed full access to her, just like any other grandmother."

Right. He had said that. And probably would do as he said. But still…

"I was clear with you from the start, Rick," she said, her heart racing. "I can't take on marriage, or full-time parenthood, either. I get claustrophobic just thinking about it."

She needed a hot bath. Someplace she could relax. She needed him on the phone, telling her what to do in the bath. Taking her away…

He was asking something of her that she just couldn't do. Under any circumstances. She had to hurt him.

And she loved him so much.

No!

Trembling, Sue promised herself she had not fallen in love with Rick Kraynick.

She wanted an aspirin. Soothing music.

"I know that's what you said, and even what you believe, but look at you, Sue. You're more of a full-time parent than anyone I've ever met. I've known you for weeks and in all that time you haven't had one hour just for you."

Yes, she had. In the tub.

"But don't you see," she said. "If I need time, have to get away, or even want to stop being a mother, all it would take is one phone call. My work's important to the system, but there are many more just like me out there, able and wanting to do what I do."

"Not according to Sonia. There's a shortage of good foster parents, and only two others in the city who can do multiple babies full-time."

Him and his statistics. His educating himself about every damn thing.

"The fact remains that if I need out, or need less, I just say so. At any point. I get that choice every single time a new baby becomes available. They ask me if I want another one, with the understanding that I can always say no."

That out allowed her to say yes. Every single time. To give. And keep giving.

Looking to the ceiling, Sue braced herself. "Oh, God, this is what I was afraid of from the very beginning," she said. And looked back at Rick. "Remember, I talked about having you give me a ring and me having to say no?"

He started to speak but she cut him off, frustrated. Desperate. "From the very beginning I told you. I'm not like most people, but that doesn't make me wrong. My life works for me. You're just like my parents, trying to make me conform."

"I don't think your life does work for you." His words, offered softly, with more compassion than anything else, weren't what she'd been expecting. "I think you have such a depth of love that you can't hold it back, which is why you're able to care for so many babies, by yourself, for years on end. What you do is amazing. Truly amazing."

He wasn't yelling at her. Telling her about her deficiencies. Not that anyone ever had.

Except herself.

"And because you have such a depth of love, I think you need the permanence you're afraid of. I think that's why I'm still in your bed. Because you finally found someone you couldn't turn away."

He'd best stop thinking. Right now. Or find himself having been in her bed for the last time.

Rick would still be her friend, wouldn't he? He'd be back. He had to be. What they had was different. Special. He felt it, too. She knew he did. And…

"I don't think the problem is your inability to care long term, or suffocating under the love of those around you."

He was just so damn sure he was right. As though he was inside her. As though he knew…

"So what do you think my problem is?" *Since you're so wise and all.*

"I think you're afraid of failing."

"What?"

"You're afraid that someone is going to need you and you aren't going to be enough. They're going to find you lacking. You're going to let them down."

Her defenses dropped out of sheer confusion. "That's

exactly right," she said, frowning. And meeting his gaze head-on. Finally. "That's what I've been saying all along."

"No, what you've been saying is that you get cramped. You have to flee because you get claustrophobic when people care for you. You suffocate under the love of others."

Yes. That was right. "And when I get that feeling, and have to have my space, I let them down. I fail them."

"Have you ever asked your parents if they feel as though you've failed them? Or have you just assumed?"

Of course she hadn't. What kind of normal family sat down and had conversations like that? There were certain things you just took for granted.

Maybe she hadn't let them down as much as she'd always believed. But there were things Rick didn't know. Things no one in her life knew. A dorm room. So much blood…

"I'm not saying I'm right, sweetie." Rick's voice entered her darkness. Pulled her back. "But is it possible that instead of your feelings of claustrophia being the cause of you failing people, it's your fear of failing people that makes you feel claustrophobic whenever they get too close? Is that possible?"

She didn't know. She honestly didn't know. And it didn't matter.

"I can't marry you," she said softly. "I'll hurt you just like Sheila did. Because, in the end it doesn't really matter which came first. The result is the same."

Rick nodded and she felt so badly.

"I'm Sheila all over again."

"No, you're not," he said, his frustration evident. "You were honest from the start. But that doesn't change the fact that I want a family. A wife. A mother for Carrie. More children. I can't settle for less."

She wanted to believe he was seeking Carrie for all the right reasons.

She wanted to be the woman he was seeking. She wanted to complete his picture.

But she was not the woman he thought he saw. She'd let him down eventually. And no mater how much her heart was breaking—it was still better to let him go now rather than hurt him so much worse later.

"And I still can't marry you," she whispered, finally finding the strength to tell him.

WHAT A BUNCH OF HOOEY. *He couldn't settle for less.* What in the hell had he been thinking? Settle for less than what? Nothing? Because that's exactly what he had all alone in his house.

Before Sue.

She'd brought him back to life.

Her and Carrie.

He'd get Carrie. He had to get Carrie. But that would still leave him without Sue.

In any capacity.

And waiting for her to see the miraculous sense in his words, to come begging him to give her another chance, to tell him that she'd seen he was right, and ask him to please marry her, was about as stupid as his great exit line.

Three days without her and he was lonely as hell.

He'd settled for less, all right. Less than the first happiness he'd known since Hannah's death.

He still hadn't cleaned Hannah's things out of the spare room. He was waiting for Sue. He wanted her to see it all. To share the memories with him.

Sitting in his kitchen, dressed in sweats and a T-shirt without the sling, Rick was ready to go out for a run. Except that he'd been ready for a couple of hours and hadn't gone. He heard a knock on his front door, and immediately thought of Sue. As though she could read his thoughts. As though his prayers had been answered.

He didn't recognize the newer looking compact car out front. Or the short-haired, nicely dressed woman on his porch when he opened the door.

"Ricky?"

He froze. He knew the voice. But it couldn't be. "Mom?"

"Yeah." With a self-deprecating smile, she glanced down at herself and then back up. "Kind of a surprise, huh? Quite the change."

She'd been sober before. Many times. For weeks, months, even a year once. But she didn't just look sober today. She looked...clean. Healthy.

Standing there blocking the doorway, he stared. "You always were good at looking the part...."

She stiffened, but managed to keep her smile. "I discovered that if you stay sober long enough, you actually get your skin tone back."

He wasn't going to feel guilty for hurting her. He wasn't going to feel anything. He couldn't.

"How long have you been sober?" he asked, hating his weakness, hating that he showed any interest at all. He'd almost added, "This time."

"Three years."

What?

"I haven't used anything hard or illegal since the first time I saw Christy high."

"I was told you checked into rehab after Carrie was born."

"I did. I'd dried out by myself, so while I wasn't using hard stuff, I wasn't completely clean, either. When I first quit, I figured I'd been through the process so many times, I didn't need the program. I got a friend to sit with me through the withdrawals, to help me do that part without medication. You know…" She just kept talking, as though he didn't have her standing out on his front porch. As though, if she stopped, she'd lose this chance. As though she knew that as soon as she let him get a word in, he was going to tell her to leave.

"…part of my problem was that those programs, they make you feel like you have to be perfect, and I knew I never could be. I never trusted myself to succeed. I never believed I would. When I did it on my own, I didn't ask me to be perfect. Just to stay off the hard stuff. Alcohol and illegal substances. When Carrie was born, I was sober, but still smoking almost five packs of cigarettes a day and relying on over-the-counter sleeping pills several times a month. I figured with only cigarettes and occasional sleeping pills to beat, and with a granddaughter who needed me because I'd failed her mother, I could damn well *be* perfect."

Oh, God. Don't do this. Please don't do this. Don't make me hope again. Don't make me want to help. Don't make me believe.

Reaching out with his good arm, Rick pulled the woman who'd borne him into his home.

CHAPTER TWENTY

SUE WASN'T DOING SO WELL. As a matter of fact, she'd been crying on and off for three days. Crying, but only when her charges were asleep. When they didn't need her. She'd called Belle but so far her cousin had had no luck connecting with Adam and Joe. Joe didn't return her calls. Adam left a message that he'd called but nothing else.

She spent the days alone with her charges. But not once, during all those long hours since Rick had left, had she felt pressured by the babies' needs. Or needed to escape their demand on her time and emotions.

No, she'd just loved them more. Because she knew she could send them back if she had to.

Rick just didn't get it. And she couldn't blame him. Some days, she didn't get it, either. He was right about one thing. She loved deeply. She'd loved every single one of her babies. Could still name them all, in order. She just had an all-in blockage. Emotionally, she needed to be independent. Distant.

Just like Joe was.

Probably because of Robert.

They must have some chemical abnormality in their emotion genes.

But, hey, it was Saturday and the sun was shining, and Jake's bruises were gone. She still had Carrie.

Deciding that a trip to the ocean was in order, Sue changed her T-shirt for a sweatshirt, and bundled up the infants. She was just loading the car when her cell phone rang.

Her mother.

She almost ignored the call. Mom would leave a message. She could call her back after some fresh ocean air cleaned her spirits.

But, really, what would it take out of her to answer now? This was her mother, for God's sake.

"Hello?"

"Sue? Oh, thank God." Her mother's anxiety reached her all the way from Florida.

"What's up?" Sue put up the blockades. Walled herself off.

"It's Adam, honey. He's had a stroke." Sue dropped to the front seat—her heart pounding as her mother named the hospital where they'd taken her newfound brother. "Daddy and I are on our way, but I was hoping you could get a sitter and go on over, sweetie. In case he doesn't…"

"And to keep us filled in until we get there." Luke took up for his wife.

Adam? He was awfully young to have a stroke. They hadn't even had a chance to get to know him. Surely he would be okay. Fate wouldn't be so cruel as to give them family and then snatch it away so quickly. The thoughts chased themselves across Sue's mind.

"I'll call Barb," she said, looking down the driveway. And then added, "Don't worry, Mom, I'll get there. And I'll phone as soon as I see him. Or a doctor. Or know more. I'll call you as soon as I'm at the hospital."

She hung up, thankful that she'd already been on her way out, with the babies safely in their car seats.

It was only after she'd dropped Carrie and Jake at Barb's that the full ramification of her mother's news hit her. Adam Fraser wasn't just her mother's brother.

He was Joe's father.

"RICKY, I DIDN'T JUST come here because of the stuff with Carrie." They were in his kitchen, drinking iced tea. His mother had been asking him questions about his job. About friends she remembered he'd had that he hadn't even known she knew. He'd been trying to talk about his niece, about the current issues between him and his mother. Trying to find a solution that would satisfy her, but that he could live with. Such as she'd give him custody, but be able to visit whenever she wanted.

She seemed so genuine. Healthier than he'd ever seen her.

But he'd believed in her so many times before. For so many different reasons.

"I know about Hannah."

His first instinct was to wipe his daughter's name off her lips. And then he looked her in the eye. And had to swallow before he could speak.

"Sonia told you." It was all he could say. As if it mattered how Nancy had found out she'd had a granddaughter she'd never met. One who could have known her sober.

One who could have bridged the chasm between them, and given Christy the family she'd so obviously needed.

"Yes." Nancy continued to hold his gaze through the tears in her eyes. "Son, I'm sorry. So, so sorry. You were always such a good boy. So bighearted and believing in me even when no one else did, swearing that I was sober when I wasn't, so they wouldn't take you away from me again. Holding my head when I was sick. Telling me I could make it when I didn't believe in myself…."

At first, Rick didn't understand what she was talking about. And then, slowly, memories started to surface. Years of moments that he'd forgotten.

"I wanted to believe you'd found the love you wanted, that you had a wonderful family who adored you. You deserve no less than that."

He wasn't sure about that. He was a guy like any other. He got angry. Said stupid things. Let people down.

"I've been through some rough times in this life," she told him. "And what I know for certain is that there's no hell worse than losing a child…."

Rick looked into her eyes and saw his own anguish. He saw himself. Someone so filled with pain even breathing was a struggle. Someone who had the strength to take the next step anyway. And the next.

Just as she'd always done. In spite of her demons. Just as she'd taught him to do.

"I wish I could have known her. And even more, I wish I could have been here for you when you lost her." Tears ran down her cheeks. And then his. He reached for his mother's hand.

"Would you like to see her room?"

ADAM FRASER WAS IN intensive care. He was allowed only two visitors at a time. Sue had to call down to the nurse's station from outside the unit. And was told there was already someone in with him. The nurse buzzed her into the unit and directed her to the family waiting room.

Belle and Emily were already there. Emily sat in a far corner, flipping too quickly through a magazine to be reading. "We don't know anything yet," Belle told Sue as she met her at the door. "Joe's in with him now. Dad's on his way," she finished with a grimace.

Tense, afraid for her mother, for Joe—and for a man she barely knew—Sue quickly perused the room. They had it to themselves. Until a man with dark red hair walked in behind her. He was dressed casually, in jeans and a flannel shirt, and she was certain she'd never seen him before. Yet she felt as though she had. There was something familiar about him. His eyes, maybe?

He caught her staring at him. And abruptly turned his back on the room to study a nutrition chart hanging on the wall.

With another glance at her aunt in the corner, Sue said, "Your mother hasn't stopped at a page since I've been here. She just keeps flipping...."

"Through one magazine after another. Yeah, she's worried about Adam. And about what Dad's going to do—or say—when he gets here."

"He hasn't come to his senses yet about Adam?"

"Not at all. If anything, he's getting more agitated by the whole thing."

Uncle Sam and agitation were not a good combination. Sue looked at her aunt and wondered, not for the first time, why she put up with Sam. Why she stayed married to him. Especially now that Belle was out of the house. Emily couldn't have an easy life.

Footsteps in the hall interrupted her thoughts, and she and Belle turned together.

"Joe!" Sue hurried forward, took both of her friend's—cousin's—hands. "How is he? How are you?"

"They don't know anything yet," Joe said to a place slightly to the right of her left ear. "He's still unconscious. But all preliminary tests look good. His heart appears to be fine. Blood's a little thick, but nothing alarming. There's brain activity. But they won't really know the extent of any damage until he wakes up."

He pulled his hands away. "And I'm fine…. Daniel?" As he spotted the other man in the waiting room, Joe left her immediately. "Hey, brother. Good to see you." The men exchanged a half handshake, half hug.

The cold, detached man was Daniel Fraser? Joe's idol when they were growing up. Adam's younger brother by twenty years. Which made him, what, thirty-eight now?

And Sue's uncle.

"How is he?" she heard Daniel ask before the two men walked out into the hall.

"Who was that?" Belle asked, coming up beside her.

"My uncle Daniel." Her uncle. Not Belle's. It was all so confusing.

After telling Belle everything she knew about Adam, Sue called her parents and left a message they could retrieve as soon as they got off the plane.

As she hung up, Daniel came back into the room. Joe didn't.

AN HOUR LATER, Sue was still sitting in the room with her family, waiting to hear anything at all about Adam. The longer he was unresponsive, the more grim the room became.

She'd tried to speak with Daniel, had introduced herself, but he'd been more reticent than Joe.

So the family trait must have come from Jo, not Robert.

And was still in Sue's blood.

Sam certainly didn't suffer from any such dysfunction. He'd talked to everyone. Including every doctor and nurse who had the misfortune to cross his path. He wanted answers, and he wanted them immediately.

That was his half brother in there. He had to know if he was going to make it.

"Yeah, wouldn't that just work out fine for him if Uncle Adam dies?" Belle whispered to Sue as they shared a small couch after Joe's latest return to tell them there'd been no change. "He could save himself attorney's fees."

Because then he'd be the only Carson son.

Like that was going to get him something he didn't already have.

With her uncle Sam reminding her of a vulture circling, waiting for death, and Joe either pacing the hall or sitting in with his unconscious father, Sue was tempted to call her dad to delay her mother's arrival at the hospital. Jenny wasn't as good at dealing with tension as Sue was.

And she thought about calling Rick. Except that there was no reason to. It seemed as though he should be made aware that she was there, sitting in vigil for the uncle she barely knew, but she couldn't come up with a logical reason for calling him. He'd made his feelings for her clear three nights before.

Either she married him or he was through. She hadn't heard from him since.

Joe was out in the hall again, speaking with an older doctor. His face grew more and more sober as he listened to something the man said. He nodded. Nodded again. And without a smile, went back toward his father's room.

And it hit her: Joe was really scared he was going to lose his father. He might think he couldn't stand the man, but he was staying right by his side as though he could somehow pull him through this crisis. Or wanted to be present in case there were going to be any lucid moments left in Adam's life.

Joe might be distant. He might be independent and reticent. But he cared.

Waiting to hear from her parents that they'd landed, and later as she sat with them in the quiet waiting room, Sue thought about her grandfather. By birth as well as by adoption. He'd brought them all there together. Her and Belle. And Adam and Sam. And Joe. He hadn't fathered Daniel, but the woman who'd had two of his children had.

He'd fathered his children in an untraditional way. He'd been unable to raise them as a family—or incapable of doing so? But here they were, all together.

She thought of the choices he'd made and hoped they were sacrifices, even if that meant the decisions had led to agony for the father of three children who had only raised one as his own. And one as his adopted child.

How he had felt about sleeping with two women at the same time, she couldn't even fathom.

Not just any two women, but his wife and his best friend's widow.

He'd lost his innocence in the war. His best friend right afterward. Had it unhinged him? Was that why he'd been so distant?

As she pulled into Barb's drive later that afternoon, with still no word about Adam, Sue had a feeling she was never going to know the answers to the questions that haunted her.

CHAPTER TWENTY-ONE

RICK SAT WITH HIS MOTHER in Sonia's office Monday morning, ready to accept whatever decision the agency had reached.

"How you doing?" he asked Nancy, giving her hand on the arm of the chair next to him a squeeze.

"I'm good." She smiled at him, squeezed back. "I'm the best I've ever been, Ricky. Yesterday, having you in my home, meeting the Franks, I didn't think that day would ever happen."

"I liked them," he told her, referring to the pastor and his wife, who rented to Nancy. "They seem genuinely kind."

"They are. Christy was about ten when I met them. Bonnie Frank is the friend who sat with me during the worst of the withdrawals."

He still couldn't believe it. That this woman was his mother. But he was working on it.

"I'm okay with however this goes today. I...she'll be fine with you," he told her, and she smiled again. "You'll just have to get used to having me hanging around the place, butting in...."

"Good morning!" Sonia breezed in, put down a folder, sat. Hands clasped on top of her desk, she made eye contact with each of them, a huge grin on her face. And when she turned to his mother, Rick knew he'd lost.

He barely heard the social worker's spiel about policies and laws and regulations, trial placement and monitoring, for the disappointment crashing through him. A disappointment far worse than he'd expected. He'd told his mother that Carrie would be fine with her, and he believed it now. If something horrible happened and Nancy faltered, Rick would be there to pick up the pieces. As would the Franks. Nancy had something now that she'd never had before. A support system. And self-confidence. Things he couldn't have understood when he was younger. Things he couldn't have given her.

"After the sixth-month period, assuming all is well, the adoption is pretty much a given, and happens quickly. The judge will…"

Carrie would be fine. But he wished she could be his little girl. Live in his home. Wished he could be the one to carry her to bed each night, to hear her prayers and kiss her good-night. To see her frown over a math problem, vegetate in front of the television on a lazy day. Wished he could teach her how to play softball, and guard her against all the boys. Hear her giggle and watch her grow. Minute by minute.

Carrie. Not Hannah. Because she was his baby sister's little girl. Because she was Carrie. An innocent baby whose smile made his world right.

And he wished Sue could be there with them. Mothering Carrie for the rest of her life.

He wished she was with him now.

"So, you're sure?" Sonia was looking at Nancy.

"Absolutely positive. My son is an incredible father. A rare combination of nurturing and strength. And this is the best thing I, or anyone, could do for Carrie. No matter what pressures might come along, my son will stand up to them, and be there for Carrie. He'll love her with everything he has. That's my Ricky." She smiled at him, tears in her eyes. And then she took his hand. "Just like he did for me."

Glancing from his mother to Sonia, Rick asked, "What's going on?"

"Your mother called me on Saturday," the caseworker said.

"I had my chances, Ricky," Nancy told him, without any bitterness in her voice. "I didn't do so hot as a mother, so I'm going to try my hand at being the best damn grandmother a little girl could ever have."

He stared at her. And then back at Sonia. "Are you saying…"

Her grin now as wide as her office, Sonia nodded and stood, holding out her hand to him. "You're going to be a daddy, Mr. Kraynick. Congratulations!"

WHEN HER PHONE RANG on Monday morning Sue wasn't prepared to see Rick's number pop up. She hadn't heard from him since she'd turned down his proposal on Wednesday. And he was supposed to be at work.

She picked up immediately. "Hi." He'd be coming

over in a matter of hours. Six—not that she was counting. To see Carrie.

He asked how Sue was. She didn't tell him she'd been rehearsing the conversation she was going to have with him since he'd walked out of her house. She'd been too harsh. Too absolute. How did she know what the future would bring her? How it might change her? "I'm fine," she said, but it wasn't true. "How about you? How's the shoulder?"

"A bit stiff, but I'm working on it."

"Overworking it, most likely. They said it could take a couple of months or more to heal."

"Or it could be fused within a couple of weeks," he reminded her. "How are the kids? I've missed them."

"They're fine. I think they miss you, too. You should have seen them when I picked them up from Barb's on Saturday. You'd think I'd left them for days instead of hours…."

"You took them to Barb's?" Was that possessiveness she heard in his voice? Even a little bit?

"My uncle Adam had a stroke."

"I…how is he?"

"He's conscious. He can move. But I guess there might be some other things going on. Liver related. They were going to do tests this morning and then we'd know more."

"I'm sorry."

She was, too. For so many things.

"It could have been worse. We could have lost him. And I've had some time to visit with my folks. They stayed here last night."

"They did?"

"Yeah."

"How did that go?"

"Well, actually. We played cards. Watched a movie. It was fun." If she didn't consider how badly she'd been missing Rick, how scared she was that she'd ruined things between them, and how guilty she felt for all the years of resenting her parents.

Someday, if she could ever grow up enough, she was going to tell them that. Apologize. And thank them.

"Listen, the reason I'm calling is…"

He paused and her heart started to pound.

"…I wanted to tell you before Sonia did. It seemed, considering, you know, me and you…it just seemed the right thing to do."

"What's going on?" She hoped she sounded at least somewhat normal, while her brain kept telling her, *Here it comes.*

"We'll be coming by together this afternoon."

"Okay." A social worker supervising a visit was not uncommon.

"To get Carrie."

"What?"

"I've been given placement."

Sue shut down. Just like that. That unnatural calm that settled in when things were too much for emotions to handle. Almost as an outside observer she watched herself.

"Congratulations!" She gave the appropriate response.

"I know you don't approve, but…"

"Actually, you're wrong about that, Rick," she

replied, glad to have an honest reply that was also a rational thing to say. "I've told you all along that I would be at peace with the agency's decision. They're trained and I trust them. I just couldn't influence them on your behalf. Besides, I've seen you with Carrie." She was babbling. "Even a fool can tell that you're an excellent father. I also thought your mother was a good choice—all right, a better choice—because she obviously wanted Carrie so badly. And my biggest fear was that you... were only going after Carrie so your mother wouldn't get her. That you were only trying to replace Hannah. I'm sorry."

"I'm taking her home with me today."

"Okay." Funny how a heart could break so quietly.

"Sonia's going to call you, but I just wanted to let you know, personally...."

"Thank you. I'll have her ready." Sue hung up. Stood for a moment to catch her breath. To organize herself. That was it, then. She took a step toward Carrie's room. Tried to remember which toys the little girl favored. And started to cry.

She'd known Carrie would be leaving her eventually. She'd always known.

She just hadn't figured on losing her heart in the process.

Rick had gained a daughter. And Sue had lost a family. Again.

SUE WAS LOSING IT. Part of her was rational enough to recognize that fact. And to rein herself in. She put on some visiting clothes—navy pants, a white blouse and blue-and-white flip-flops. She left her hair down. Because it looked more professional, not because Rick liked it that way.

She wore a dab of old makeup. To cover the evidence of tears.

Carrie had a big lunch. A long nap. A bath. And was wearing a dress Sue's mom had brought for her from Florida. It was light gray with small white polka dots, a white rounded collar and a little pink bow at the breast. It went beautifully with Carrie's baby-soft dark hair.

Her parents were staying at a hotel in the city that night to be close to the hospital. Maybe she should call them. See if they wanted company. With only one baby, she'd be practically traveling alone.

She'd like to see Uncle Adam. Her mother said he'd been talking some. And had been glad she'd come….

Rick's Nitro pulled up the drive.

This was it.

Checking to see that Jake was fine in the swing, she picked up Carrie. Walked with her to the door, ready to greet the baby's new family.

Just as she always did when turning over one of her charges. It didn't take long. A few minutes max. The new parents were always eager to get this foster part of their lives behind them and start being a real family.

She had the door open by the time they got to the walk. Seeing Rick, Carrie started bouncing against Sue's hip. The baby grinned and, as he approached, reached for him.

"Hi, princess, Daddy's come to get you," he said, holding out both arms to her.

Sue could see Sonia behind Rick. And Nancy, too.

She knew the ropes. Had played her part many, many times. Had it down pat.

But when Rick reached for his new daughter, Sue didn't let the baby go.

SOMETHING WAS WRONG. Horribly wrong. One glance in Sue's frantic eyes and he knew that he had to act.

"How's my punkin'?" He continued to croon to the baby without missing a beat, holding on to Sue's hand with his own, as if he'd meant all along to grab her hand, not to take the baby from her. Then, with his good arm around Carrie's foster mother, and his other hand still at the baby's bottom, he stepped back into Sue's foyer.

She continued to look at him, pleading with her eyes. And he turned.

"Sonia? Mom? Do you care if we take a few minutes to ourselves, first? There's something I need to discuss with Sue."

Sonia blinked. Looked from him to Sue. And then she nodded. "Nancy and I can have a cup of coffee and talk about ways she could volunteer at the agency, if that's all right with you?" The counselor glanced at his mother.

"Of course."

"We'll be back in an hour," Sonia said, and turned from the door.

Certain that what had just happened was highly inappropriate, Rick made a mental note to thank the counselor for putting humanity above her job. Obviously, the baby was safe. She was with two agency-approved caregivers.

And sometimes life was bigger than rules and regulations.

SUE HEARD RICK GET RID OF the others. She knew they were alone. And still she couldn't release her grip on Carrie.

"Sue?" He led her to the couch. Sat with her, his arm still around her. One finger locked in Carrie's grip. "Talk to me, sweetie."

The baby, as though sensing that something monumental was happening, began to fidget.

"I…" Sue was going to give him her usual answer. An assurance that she was fine and could handle anything. She was Sue Bookman. The strong one. The family go-to girl. The one who needed her independence. Her space.

"Oh, God, Rick…" She started to cry. And then to sob. Ugly, wrenching bursts.

Rick reached for Carrie. "I'm not taking her away from you, I'm just moving her over to her swing so Jake doesn't get lonely."

She had to let the baby go. For Carrie's sake. And Jake's. The babies always came first.

Bereft without the little girl in her arms, Sue bent over, her arms around her middle, her head to her knees.

With gut-wrenching sobs, she was drowning in the release of a decade of pent-up anguish.

The couch depressed beneath Rick's weight. He rubbed her back, his voice soothing, though she wasn't sure what he was saying. If he was saying anything besides promising her she wasn't alone. Telling her he was there.

She cried until her ribs hurt, and kept on. Until she didn't think she was ever going to stop.

Which was why she'd always been afraid to start.

When she started to choke, Rick pulled her onto his lap, cradling her like one of her charges, bearing most of her weight with his right arm. With his left, he smoothed hair away from her face. Ran a finger along her neck. Her shoulder. He started to notice the little things. "Come on, sweetie. Talk to me."

"Oh, Rick." She shuddered. Picked at a string coming loose from one of the buttons on his shirt, while tears dripped down her cheeks. "I…can't tell you."

"Of course you can." Taking hold of her chin, he made her look at him. "This is me, Rick, remember? I'm the guy who understands that you'll never give him your whole self, but who just keeps coming back anyway."

"I was a jerk."

"Berating yourself isn't going to do anyone any good," he said now. "I just need to know what this is about."

Sue could hear Grandma, telling her that all she had to do was speak her heart. To be honest.

Grandma, who'd kept secrets.

And that was wrong. Secrets hurt.

"I had a baby...."

The words, stark and cold and unfamiliar, hurt just coming out of her mouth.

Rick quieted. His hand slowed where he'd been rubbing her shoulder. His breathing, even his heartbeat beneath her cheek, seemed to revert to slow motion.

She wanted to rest. To sleep for a good long time.

"When?"

Rick's question was fair. And what did it matter, now, if he knew? Her secret was out.

"Almost ten years ago." She started to cry again when she'd thought she was done. Joe's daughter, Kaitlin, was ten.

"Did you give it up for adoption?" That was the obvious conclusion.

She shook her head. "No." She had to stop her voice from shaking. Her mind from working.

"Tell me about your baby, honey." His voice was kind. Compassionate. And demanding, too. "Tell me what happened."

"I—it—I..." She was on the floor, hard tile, cold. All she could see was a toilet. And blood. So much blood.

"Sue?"

Rick's concern stopped her tears. Stopped everything. "I was young and stupid," she said, her voice thick from crying so much. And then, barely above a whisper, she continued, "The night Joe got married, I slept with this guy. It was horrible. Painful. Degrading. I'd never really even made out with anyone before. When it was over I just wanted to put the whole thing behind me. The guy was long gone. He'd been a visitor to campus, someone I met at a party. I didn't even know his full name. And he never tried to contact me again afterward. And then a couple of months later, I realized I was pregnant. I didn't tell anyone. Couldn't. I was barely eighteen. In my freshman year at State. I couldn't raise a child on my own, with no way of finding the father…not that I wanted to. If I told my parents they'd make me come home and my life would be over. I decided to have the baby in secrecy—somehow—give it up for adoption, and go on with my life and they'd never know."

"That didn't happen?"

She shook her head. "I was in this physical fitness class and we were required to jog three times a week. Since I hadn't told anyone I was pregnant, I jogged."

"Didn't your doctor tell you that was dangerous?"

"I didn't have a doctor."

His silence said a lot.

"I killed my baby, Rick."

"You did not kill it."

"I started to cramp really bad one afternoon after I got back to my dorm from jogging. I tried to call for help, but the pain was so bad, I couldn't make it to the door. I lost the baby on the bathroom floor."

Now that she needed to cry, her tears were all dried up. Along with her heart. He knew now why she could

never, ever be trusted to love enough. Why she didn't
deserve all-in love from anyone.

"All alone." His two words said it all.

"Yes."

"How far along were you?"

"Five months." Enough to be able to tell… "It was
a girl."

A girl. Finally, the dam broke again. Sue sobbed
more quietly this time. Mourning what she'd lost. Her
daughter. Herself.

Rick just held her. Let her cry.

"Eventually…" she said, sniffling, "…I was able to
get to my phone. Dial 911."

"And did they tell you at the hospital that a lot of
women jog while they're pregnant?"

She shook her head. "They said that wasn't neces-
sarily the reason I lost her, but it was. It happened right
after I got back. Women can jog when they're pregnant
so long as their pregnancies are progressing normally.
And generally only if they'd jogged before getting
pregnant. I was five months pregnant, and I hadn't
even seen a doctor. I killed her, Rick. Killed her with
negligence."

"No, Sue, chances are you'd have lost the baby,
anyway. It just happens sometimes. A life that isn't meant
to be. You didn't kill anyone. You were a frightened young
girl who was in over her head and needed help at a time
when you felt there was no one around to help you."

She'd lost her best friend—her only real friend—
when she'd rejected Joe.

"It was a miscarriage, Sue. Plain and simple. Twenty percent of women who are pregnant miscarry."

Rick and his statistics. Remembered from the birth of his own daughter over seven years ago? Having a walking encyclopedia around was kind of nice.

"The tragedy is that you were so young. And alone. And didn't get help to deal with your loss."

"I felt responsible. Guilty."

"Didn't they tell you in the emergency room that it wasn't your fault?"

"Yeah. And my ob-gyn told me later, too. But I knew better."

When Rick chuckled, a world that had turned sickeningly off-kilter righted itself enough for Sue to take in a full deep breath. "That's my Sue," he said. "She knows better."

"Sometimes I do."

"Most times you do. That's what makes it so dangerous those few times you don't."

"I think I've solved the chicken and egg thing with my claustrophobia," she said softly, not wanting to sit up, to move her face away from his chest.

"Which came first?"

"My fear of failure."

"Mix that with my aversion to believing anyone is going to stay in my life for the long haul and we make quite a pair."

And Sue realized something else. She hadn't just pushed Rick away. He'd been waiting to be abandoned. To be let go.

"I know you've got this thing about second chances," she ventured, "but I was wondering if I could have a redo."

"On what?"

"Last Wednesday night. Right after you asked me to marry you. For Carrie's sake."

"Depends on what your answer's going to be this time around."

His voice rumbling beneath her chest was a comfort. And exciting. To be understood, fully understood, and still not be alone…

Suddenly life had possibilities. The grief wasn't going to go away. For either of them. But neither of them would be bearing it alone….

"My answer would be no, I won't marry you for Carrie's sake. But if you can change your question, I might change my mind."

Rick held her away from him, staring down at her, deadly serious. "I love you, Sue Bookman. I want you to be my wife. I want to raise our daughter, to make more babies with you, and to continue to love those children that need our love for as long as they need us. My question is, do you want what I want?"

With tears in her eyes, careful of his sore shoulder, Sue crawled up Rick's chest until her mouth was an inch from his. "Yes, Rick. Oh, yes, I love you, too. And I want the same things you do…."

Just as their lips met, Carrie screamed for attention and woke Jake up.

"Starting now?" Sue asked, moving on his lap.

"Starting now."

Holding hands, with a promise in their shared glance for more intimacy later that night, they moved as one to care for the children.

THE DOORBELL STARTLED them both. "Sonia," Rick said, watching as Sue finished securing Carrie's diaper. He picked up Jake, who'd also just been changed. "Let's go, little man." Settling Jake in his left arm, which bore the weight without pain, he pulled Sue up against him with the other and walked her to the door, eager to introduce her as his wife-to-be.

"We haven't said where we're going to be living." Just like Sue, always thinking ahead.

"I like it out here."

"I don't want to have to do without you for long drives to work every day."

"So we can live at my house." And then he remembered something else. "I have a room I want you to help me dismantle."

With a gentle kiss, and a look in her eyes he hadn't dared believe he'd ever see, Sue said, "I'd be honored," and pulled open her front door.

"Mom! Dad! I was going to call you."

Openmouthed, Jenny gaped, saying absolutely nothing for once. Luke stared down the tall man in his daughter's home, with an arm around her and a baby in his other arm.

"It's about damn time." He held out his hand.

With his own hand suddenly engulfed in a firm grip, Rick grinned and knew he'd just gained a dad. His first ever.

Which just went to show that if a man lived long enough, he could have everything.

IT WASN'T UNTIL MUCH later that night, after Sonia and Nancy had come back, joined in the festivities and left, that Sue's parents told her the reason for their impromptu visit. The four of them had put the babies to bed and ordered pizza. Jenny had heard from Emily that Adam's preliminary results looked good. And now they were sitting in the living room.

Jenny pulled an old familiar box out of her purse. Sue didn't want to look at it. Didn't want to see it anywhere but on Grandma's dresser. She'd had enough for one day.

"I need you to keep this for me, sweetie, please," her mom said, handing the box to Sue.

When she didn't immediately reach for it, Rick did, holding it in both hands as he sat next to her on the couch. He was so close their thighs were touching, and for the first time in her life Sue had a glimpse of what it was going to be like to have someone share everything in life with her. And fully understood what perfect moments were all about.

She stared at the box.

"I've got that weak spot where your uncle Sam's concerned," her mother said.

"He just won't let up on Jenny about the necklace. He calls her almost every day. Sends e-mails," Luke added.

"Does he know you have it with you?"

"No," Jenny said. "But he's mentioned it several times. I'm afraid, if I keep it, I'm going to give in to him."

"I think it's a good idea for you to keep it, Sue," Luke explained. "Sam won't be able to get it from your mother, and he won't know to come to you."

"And even if he did, he'd never, ever get it from me," Sue said. She was a strong woman. She could count on herself.

But she needed people, too.

"What does Sam want with this?" Rick asked, indicating the box.

"Probably to sell it," Sue said. "It's been in our family for generations. Losing it to my uncle's avariciousness would be criminal. Horrible."

"I think he wants it to solidify his right to it," Jenny said. "Being the only child of Robert and Sarah, being ruler of the family, seems to be his driving force. I've just never been able to figure out why."

Sue wished her mother would quit trying. And yet she took an odd comfort in the fact that she knew Jenny wouldn't. Because that was who she was.

The woman who'd given Sue life. Who'd always been her champion. Her support. Whose greatest sin was in wanting Sue to always know that she was loved.

Thinking of Carrie asleep in her crib, Sue hoped that someday she could be half the mother Jenny Bookman was.

The four of them talked long into the night. About Adam and Joe. Sarah, Robert and Jo. About Daniel— Jo's child with her second husband—so set apart.

About Nancy. And Christy. And about Hannah. Sue cried as her husband-to-be told her parents about the daughter he'd lost.

And she loved her parents so much when they asked if they could visit the girl's grave with them before they flew home the next day.

Trying to understand, they talked about Jo giving Jenny away. About Robert continuing his affair with Jo after Adam was born. About Rick's mom unable to sign away her rights to her son so he could be adopted. And Christy, who'd ended her own life. They wondered, in the quiet safety of their small circle, if things might have been different, better, had one person done one thing differently.

And in the end, they could only find one answer. Love. Love brought understanding. It brought forgiveness. It held families together, brought them together. And as long as there was family, there would be love.

Rick slid the box on his lap between Sue's hand and his, pushing it into her palm. "You haven't looked at this."

"I know."

"Maybe you should."

She stared at the box. Wanted to hide it in a bottom drawer and forget about it. Just as she'd tried to forget that bathroom floor so many years ago.

Sue opened the box. And stared at the marvelously intricate gold chain with the heart-shaped diamond surrounded by sapphires of the purest blue.

"That's magnificent," Rick said in a near whisper. "I've never seen anything like it."

"It belongs in a museum," Luke agreed. "Except that

in this family, it's not a jewel, or a piece of art. It's the heart that holds us all together."

Through a blur of tears, Sue continued to look at the heirloom that had been at her grandmother's throat for every important family event she could remember. Graduations. Robert's retirement. Luke's retirement. Sue's mom and dad's going-away party when they moved to Florida.

Whatever else Grandma had done, whatever secrets she'd kept, she'd loved them all with her whole heart. She'd given them her whole life.

And Sarah Sue Carson was going to continue the legacy.

* * * * *

Don't miss the next book in this family saga!
Look for FOR THE LOVE OF FAMILY
by Kathleen O'Brien
in October 2009
from Harlequin Superromance.

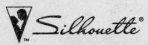

Silhouette®

Romantic
SUSPENSE

**Sparked by Danger,
Fueled by Passion.**

The Agent's Secret Baby

by *USA TODAY* bestselling author
Marie Ferrarella

TOP SECRET DELIVERIES

Dr. Eve Walters suddenly finds herself pregnant
after a regrettable one-night stand and turns to an
online chat room for support. She eventually learns
the true identity of her one-night stand: a DEA agent
with a deadly secret. Adam Serrano does not want
this baby or a relationship, but can fear for Eve's
and the baby's lives convince him that this is what
he has been searching for after all?

Available October wherever books are sold.

**Look for upcoming titles in
the TOP SECRET DELIVERIES miniseries**
The Cowboy's Secret Twins by Carla Cassidy—November
The Soldier's Secret Daughter by Cindy Dees—December

Visit Silhouette Books at www.eHarlequin.com

SRS27650

You're invited to join our Tell Harlequin Reader Panel!

By joining our new reader panel you will:

- Receive Harlequin® books—they are FREE and yours to keep with no obligation to purchase anything!
- Participate in fun online surveys
- Exchange opinions and ideas with women just like you
- Have a say in our new book ideas and help us publish the best in women's fiction

In addition, you will have a chance to win great prizes and receive special gifts! See Web site for details. Some conditions apply. Space is limited.

To join, visit us at
www.TellHarlequin.com.

REQUEST YOUR FREE BOOKS!

2 FREE NOVELS PLUS 2 FREE GIFTS!

HARLEQUIN®

Super Romance®

Exciting, emotional, unexpected!

YES! Please send me 2 FREE Harlequin® Superromance® novels and my 2 FREE gifts (gifts are worth about $10). After receiving them, if I don't wish to receive any more books, I can return the shipping statement marked "cancel." If I don't cancel, I will receive 6 brand-new novels every month and be billed just $4.69 per book in the U.S. or $5.24 per book in Canada. That's a savings of close to 15% off the cover price! It's quite a bargain! Shipping and handling is just 50¢ per book*. I understand that accepting the 2 free books and gifts places me under no obligation to buy anything. I can always return a shipment and cancel at any time. Even if I never buy another book from Harlequin, the two free books and gifts are mine to keep forever.

135 HDN EYLG   336 HDN EYLS

Name _____ (PLEASE PRINT) _____

Address _____ Apt. # _____

City _____ State/Prov. _____ Zip/Postal Code _____

Signature (if under 18, a parent or guardian must sign)

Mail to the **Harlequin Reader Service:**
IN U.S.A.: P.O. Box 1867, Buffalo, NY 14240-1867
IN CANADA: P.O. Box 609, Fort Erie, Ontario L2A 5X3
Not valid to current subscribers of Harlequin Superromance books.

**Are you a current subscriber of Harlequin Superromance books
and want to receive the larger-print edition?
Call 1-800-873-8635 today!**

* Terms and prices subject to change without notice. Prices do not include applicable taxes. Sales tax applicable in N.Y. Canadian residents will be charged applicable provincial taxes and GST. Offer not valid in Quebec. This offer is limited to one order per household. All orders subject to approval. Credit or debit balances in a customer's account(s) may be offset by any other outstanding balance owed by or to the customer. Please allow 4 to 6 weeks for delivery. Offer available while quantities last.

Your Privacy: Harlequin is committed to protecting your privacy. Our Privacy Policy is available online at www.eHarlequin.com or upon request from the Reader Service. From time to time we make our lists of customers available to reputable third parties who may have a product or service of interest to you. If you would prefer we not share your name and address, please check here. ☐

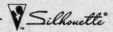

SPECIAL EDITION

FROM *NEW YORK TIMES* BESTSELLING AUTHOR

SUSAN MALLERY

DESERT ROGUES

THE SHEIK AND THE BOUGHT BRIDE

Victoria McCallan works in Prince Kateb's palace.
When Victoria's gambling father is caught cheating
at cards with the prince, Victoria saves her father from
going to jail by being Kateb's mistress for six months.
But the darkly handsome desert sheik isn't as harsh as
Victoria thinks he is, and Kateb finds himself attracted to
his new mistress. But Kateb has already loved and lost
once—is he willing to give love another try?

Available in October wherever books are sold.

SSE65481

COMING NEXT MONTH

Available October 13, 2009

#1590 FOR THE LOVE OF FAMILY • Kathleen O'Brien
The Diamond Legacy
Every family has secrets, but Belle Carson has an old one that's a doozy! Entangled with newfound relatives, Belle finds things getting more complicated when she starts falling for her new boss, Matt Malone. And now she's keeping a few secrets from him. Don't you just hate it when history repeats itself?

#1591 HIS SECRET AGENDA • Beth Andrews
Dean can't fall for Allie Martin—he's working her! And when the ex-lawyer finds out that Dean Garret's not the laid-back cowboy bartender she hired, their passion could turn from love to hate as fast as it takes him to whip up a margarita....

#1592 MADISON'S CHILDREN • Linda Warren
The Belles of Texas
Madison Belle can't have children and is resigned to the single life. Until she meets Walker, the law of High Cotton, Texas, and his two adorable kids. She's falling in love and life is perfect, until his ex-wife shows up...carrying his child.

#1593 HER BEST BET • Pamela Ford
When Izzy Gordon's friend bets her there's no way she'll marry her oh-so-perfect boyfriend, Izzy thinks it's money in the bank. Then she meets Gib Murphy, and Izzy can't stop thinking about him. Maybe the smarter money is on Gib!

#1594 NEXT COMES LOVE • Helen Brenna
An Island to Remember
From the moment Erica Corelli steps off the ferry with a little boy in tow, Sheriff Garrett Taylor's plans for a quiet life are jeopardized. And it's not just the trouble following her. Garrett can't seem to fight the attraction igniting between them.

#1595 THE MAN SHE ONCE KNEW • Jean Brashear
Going Back
Callie Hunter would give anything not to be back in this town. Still, she has a duty to do, so here she is. Not much has changed...except for David Langley—the first boy she loved. This David bears little resemblance to the one she knew, but it seems her heart doesn't recognize the difference.

HSRCNMBPA0909